StUffED

StUffED

**BY
GORDON GRAHAM**

**DUFFY & SNELLGROVE
SYDNEY**

Published by Duffy and Snellgrove 2001
PO Box 177 Potts Point NSW 1335 Australia
info@duffyandsnellgrove.com.au

Distributed by Pan Macmillan

© Gordon Graham 2001

Cover design by Gretta Kool
Typeset by Cooper Graphics in Bembo 11/13

Printed by Griffin Press

ISBN 1 875989 85 4

visit our website: www.duffyandsnellgrove.com.au

GaRVEY QUiNN

Even now, after the way things have turned out, I know there must still be some people who look at me, remember how I was, and say, how could someone do that to himself? These days, though, they usually don't say it to my face. Sometimes I still get sniggers, but I hardly feel a thing.

People came up with all kinds of crazy ideas when they tried to understand. They thought I went to such extremes in transforming myself to play that role because I'm a perfectionist. They saw me as someone who wouldn't settle for anything less than absolute truth when he's acting, no matter how painful the personal consequences might be. No matter how ugly. They imagined that what they saw before them, when I was at my worst, was the result of my belief that no price is too great to pay when art is at stake. They thought that however appalling the outcome, however misguided my actions might have looked afterwards, I did it because I believed in something. Something more than what there is. They couldn't believe that anyone could take himself so far down the path of humiliation and pain and the annihilation of every good thing he had going for him without some kind of master plan.

They were right off the mark. I never deliberately set out to do anything except a decent job of work, or to be anything except myself. The thing is, I never had a problem with the impression people got when they saw me smiling out from the cover of *TV Week*. If they wanted to see me as just another blond prettyboy type with a big jaw and lots of muscles, that was all right by me. To me the job was mostly about making sure people liked you, and how many jobs give you that opportunity? When I was doing bar work, or some of the labouring jobs Dad steered my way, before I got the big break, in those jobs no matter how good you were, either people thought you were a complete dickhead or they couldn't give a stuff one way or the other, and what's the point of living like that?

On the other hand, though I liked it when people sent me fan mail and recognised me in the supermarket, I also tried to keep my feet firmly on the ground, which is more than you can say for some people in the business. With me, what you saw was what you got. I thought, is acting such a big deal anyway, that it's worth transforming yourself into the sort of person you wouldn't want to know, for the good of your career? What's so wrong with getting up there in front of the cameras and, basically, being who you are – only you just happen to be saying someone else's words? Plenty of people have made it big doing exactly that.

Then again, I'm not so thick I'm not aware that there's another school of thought on this. Often enough when I was in *Medical Emergency*, the show that made it happen for me, we'd have actors coming in for guest roles, what some people around the place liked to call real actors, only I wasn't buying that. They were doing their job and I was doing mine, and I was the one the audience tuned in to watch. But sometimes on the set, hanging around like you have to, hour after hour, you'd hear them talking about what they were doing. To me, you come in, you say the words like the dialogue coach has told you to, you make sure your feet line up with the bits of tape on the floor, you do your best to look good, chin out, gut in and biceps clenched, and that's basically it. And I must have been doing something right to get through three seasons. But these guys, some of them would be doing, I don't know, *Hamlet*, or Shakespeare or whatever at night, and they'd come onto *Medical Emergency* during the day to play some character who's only there for the one show, like a car crash victim or a drunken derro or a cop dying of gunshot wounds. And they're only on screen for five minutes, and you know they're only doing the job to pay the rent, but you'd hear them going on and on.

How am I going to find my character's central truth? How can I play this in a way that taps into the darkness in my own soul? What journey is this character taking, and how does this link in with my own personal journey? How can I strip away everything I believe in and capture some essential essence, blah blah blah, yadda yadda yadda and on and on and on.

Probably they'd take on any part, no matter how stupid or dorky or fucked in the head the character might be. All they want is for people to believe they've become someone else, even if that someone else is the most pathetic excuse for a human being you ever saw in your life. I knew for a fact that some of them were jealous as hell when they heard about the film I was being offered, however much they might have laughed at me later on. They wanted the part because of how far they thought they'd have to go.

So quite frankly all this serious acting talk seemed like a big wank. The only person I could cop it from was my girlfriend, Madeleine. She was another real actor, having to guest on *Medical Emergency* after the cops nabbed her for two years worth of unpaid parking fines. She had to play a stripper, bashed up by some nightclub heavies, and I had to find her, crawling across the carpark towards casualty, just as I was returning from a run in the park after my shift had finished, all rippling muscles and sweat, in that singlet I'd torn open at the sides to show a bit more pec. I scooped her up and carried her in, and our eyes met, but it was doomed love because my character knew that once he patched her up she'd be back out there into the same dangerous world, and next time they'd probably finish her for good.

Between takes, though, it was anything but doomed love. Even though Madeleine was going on about listening to her character's inner dialogue, and trying to simultaneously play the woman and the child that woman had once been, to balance her performance on that actual moment of lost innocence, I found I just wanted to listen and listen, almost like I was hypnotised. There was something about the way she sounded the words, that gave you no choice but to believe, which is the same feeling you got when you saw her acting. What she was feeling about me then I wasn't sure, but I did notice she couldn't take her eyes off my body, especially when I was swapping singlets for a re-shoot of the carpark scene.

So, when I got the phone call from Stirling Seagrave, offering me the part that would change my life, Madeleine was the first to hear about it. She was also the first to see my worried look.

Garvey, is there something wrong with you? Stirling Seagrave offers you the lead in his new movie and you stand there looking like you're in the dentist's chair?

Yeah, but he wants me to play Bryan Mars.

So what's your worry? All right, Bryan Mars was a swimmer, but with Stirling Seagrave directing, this won't be just another sports bio-pic. This will be art. It's a story for our times.

But the story's just such a downer, I tell her, wishing art

hadn't come into the conversation this early. I mean, here's a guy who had everything, the champion with the world at his feet, being looked on as practically a god after what he did. And yet he let it all slip, he ended up as just a fat joke, a bloated hopeless loser who disgraced himself in public, in fact disgraced the whole nation who'd looked up to him so much.

Just talking about it makes me sad, but somehow Madeleine's got a half-smile.

Yes. How the mighty can fall. Imagine what Shakespeare could have done with it.

But the way it ends. He just disappears into the ocean, gone without a trace, like he never existed and nothing he did was worth anything.

Sometimes when you argue with Madeleine she reacts to everything you say as if it just goes one step further towards proving her point.

Exactly.

Well I'm sorry, but I just don't buy that, I tell her. What it's really saying, is that we all end up as a handful of dust and God's got the last laugh. What audience is going to want to see that?

The audience wants to see truth.

This starts to get me angry, angrier than I've ever been with her before.

Yeah, yeah, I'm sure all your mates from drama school would kill to play Bryan Mars, all those serious actors who come on *Medical Emergency* and grunt and groan like Marlon Brando. But I happen to care what I look like.

All right Garvey, let me put it another way. If you don't go through with this, I'm leaving.

After that, I stop arguing. Madeleine goes out and gets the video of the first feature by Stirling Seagrave, the new so-called genius of the Aussie cinema, though looking back on it now, I'd have to say, genius my arse. It's called *Blood and Thunder*, which somehow I'd missed seeing first time around. Funnily enough I don't go to the movies that often, I don't want to see too much acting, I have to put up with enough of it at work during the day. Something with Arnie or Jean-Claude Van Damme in it is usually about the most I can manage. But we sat there and watched this thing of Seagrave's. It's a kind of day in the life of a mass killer and I have to say, I didn't mind it, it moved fast, it made sense, and most importantly for me, Seagrave made the people in it look good, even Johnny Hearn, who in real life is as ugly as sin. That was another reason I started to come round to the idea, because I'd heard that Johnny was really pissed off with Stirling Seagrave for not casting him. Johnny's another one of these serious guys who gives interviews where he says of course he'd never consider compromising his art by doing television shit like *Medical Emergency*, so I knew seeing me get the part would piss him off even more. Some of these types, you want to grab hold of them and shake them and shout, it's just a fucking job, mate.

So I go to this office that Seagrave operates out of, and just as you'd expect, it's on the top floor of a converted warehouse in Surry Hills, up above an art gallery full of these African statues with huge dicks. I'm led in by this girl who looks like she's about sixteen, wearing the shortest black mini skirt you've ever seen, and Seagrave's sitting back in his chair with his cowboy boots up on the desk, doesn't even get up to shake my hand, just gives this feeble little waving gesture at me to sit down. He's got a ponytail, he's got his shades on, and he's smoking a big cigar, the whole Hollywood deal, and he's wearing this long black leather coat even though it's a muggy day and the place doesn't seem to have air-conditioning. It's not a great start to our working relationship, and it gets worse right away because the first thing he says to me isn't, how you going, want a coffee, nothing like that, he just comes right out with it.

I'm going to level with you, Garvey, I'm not hiring you for your acting ability.

I still haven't been invited to take a seat, but I sit down anyway. Seagrave shuts up for a little while, like he's waiting to see how I'm going to react, but I don't say anything. I mean what is there to say to something like that? So I wait too, and he gives a kind of smirk.

What I want, he tells me, is someone who's a complete blank, someone I can mould into exactly what I want, like a lump of clay. And to be brutally frank, you're about the blankest actor I've ever seen.

Yes, I can understand, some people might have taken this as an insult, but to me it was a relief. What I was worried about before I went in was that he was going to start talking about building a character, finding the essential truth, and all the rest of it, so being told he's going to treat me like a lump of clay isn't a problem.

Well, I say, you're the director, and I see that smirk again, kind of made worse by his funny little beard that looks like he's just drawn a stripe up the middle of his chin with a texta colour.

Then we get talking about my availability, which, seeing as *Medical Emergency* got canned, is pretty flexible. What floors me is that he's talking about this film taking up a whole year. Now this might be my first feature, but I do know enough about movies to know that the actual filming bit doesn't take nearly that long. This is when I find out what's really in store for me.

Remember Robert de Niro in *Raging Bull*? he asks me.

I tell him, yeah, of course I do. I figure he's mentioning it because de Niro was playing a boxer and I'm going to be playing a swimmer, and he's going to make some point about what's involved in playing an athlete.

Remember how in the movie he changed from being the trim, muscular fighter at the beginning to the fat slob at the end? Seagrave asks me. How do you think he did that?

Padding? I answer, because to be honest the movie's not that clear in my mind. I only saw it late at night on TV over a few beers and pizza with Madeleine, and it had all this annoying opera music in it, so I might not have been concentrating. And there's that smirk again.

Do you really think they could achieve that level of reality with padding? he asks me, and I'm starting to get sick of all the questions. Why can't he just get to the point? Well, maybe not, I say.

Before he talks again, Seagrave blows out a big cloud of cigar smoke, which wafts straight over towards me. I don't know whether he's done it deliberately.

What Mr de Niro did, and what you're going to do, is train like a serious athlete for months before we start filming. When people see you in your Speedos, they'll believe you're Bryan Mars, world record holder, the superfish.

At last I've got a chance to say something that makes me look good. Not that I'm that keen to sell myself, but I'm tired of everything going his way.

You've got no worries there, I tell him. I'd have to be one of the fittest actors around, in this business it all comes down to how good you look. I work out, I run, I swim laps, so I could probably just about pass for an Olympic champ already, as a matter of fact yesterday I …

I get another cloud of smoke as Seagrave talks on, like he hasn't listened to a word I've said.

Then we film for six weeks, he tells me. The early part of Bryan Mars's career, the relentless dedication, the rise to glory, the world records, the public acclaim, the high life, the women's magazine stories, the build-up to the Olympics and the speculation, just how many gold medals can one man win?

Then the great sea rescue, the turning point of his life, the step up to superhero status and the incredible demands on him. The public appearances, the TV shows, the book deals, and then the wild scenes in nightclubs and the brawls with photographers, the anxiety about the Olympic trials. The first signs that all is not right in the world of Bryan Mars. And then we stop filming.

I can't help asking what seems like the obvious question. Why?

Seagrave looks at me like I'm an idiot.

Then you do what de Niro did. Basically you pig out. You go to seed. You stop all exercise and just lie around eating all day, heavy, fatty junk food, plus buckets of booze. A few weeks of that should pack on enough flab to get you to the stage where we can start filming again, the debacle of the Olympic trials, the sorrow and anger, the lashing out, the torn-up contracts, the shattered hopes of the man and of the nation who worshipped him. And then we stop filming again.

Because it's the end? I ask.

Again, that smirk. Just who does Seagrave think he is?

Because then we need a few more months to really go for broke, this time you eat nothing but fat, fat, fat, deep fried everything, until you look like he did at the end. The super fish has turned into a whale.

I refuse to laugh at this. I remember people making that joke at the time. I didn't think it was funny then either, though lots of people I know pissed themselves over it.

Seagrave goes on. Then the final scenes. The break-up with the gorgeous girlfriend. The come-down of going to the Olympics as a commentator. The debacle by the pool, watched by countless millions around the world. The humiliation of being sacked by the network and the lonely flight home. And finally, the little pile of clothes on the very same stormy beach where, just a year before, he performed the extraordinary feat of heroism which, ironically, was to begin his decline. And out to sea, Bryan Mars, once as sleek as a seal, but now a danger to shipping, gulps for air as he gets ready to go under for the last time.

This was what I was afraid of. All that stuff glorifying misery and failure, and who's going to want to see that? And what's worse, going by the kind of jokes Seagrave makes about the poor guy, he's going to send the whole thing up. I've also got other concerns.

But what do I do then?

Seagrave looks genuinely puzzled by my question, and takes a moment to come up with an answer.

What do you do? Get another job, I suppose. Whatever you want to do.

No, I mean, about the fat?

Now Seagrave laughs, like there's something funny about me for not knowing the answer already.

We give you a personal trainer. It'll be in your contract. You train your butt off and in a few months more you'll be back to being good old Garvey Quinn.

I can't believe it's quite that easy. I've never had a weight problem myself, because there's never been a time when I haven't been doing something physical, right on from school where I was always mad on footy and cricket, and a couple of years in the juniors with my brother Dean, always in the surf a lot, then into gym work when my career took off and it was important for my pecs to look good. I've just always been a very physical guy. But I've seen people who've let themselves go a bit, actors on the show who've got into the big lunch scene and everything, waiting for the big break and thinking they'll get it by accepting every lunch invite that comes up, and then on to the pub afterwards to tell their mates how lunch went and knock a few beers back, and suddenly they're five kilos overweight and nobody wants to know them. Then of course you see them in the gym, busting a gut, and it's painful to see, the look of desperation when the scales still tell them exactly the same thing and the workouts just get harder and harder. We're talking about full-scale agony over a few kilos, so what's it going to be like for me with the sort of blow-out Seagrave's talking about?

I'm a bit worried. I tell him, you make it sound easy, but I'm not sure –

Somehow this is funny to him, and he splutters on the word easy as he says it back to me. Easy? I never used the word easy. Do you think great art is easy?

Once he starts talking about art, I know I'm in deep shit.

I just mean that, well, it's my body we're talking about here, and to do that sort of thing to yourself –

So, you think you're better than Robert de Niro, do you?

Now if there's one thing I can't stand it's people putting words into my mouth. This is where I give myself one last chance not to do something that could change my entire life, in a way that I might not like.

Mind if I think about this for twenty-four hours?

★ ★ ★

Immediately afterwards I go to see Stuie Fengler, my agent, in the garage he uses for an office. He doesn't say a thing as he lets me in through the roller door and leads me past his old Lada Samara that everybody makes jokes about, and I can tell that he's worried. Stuie's so short that when he sits down at his desk he almost disappears behind it, about all you can see is his little bald head and the few strands of blond hair he combs over it at about 45 degrees. He stares at me for a while like there's a lot hanging on what I've got to tell him and if it's bad news he doesn't want to hear it. Finally he asks.

So, how did it go?

I told him I wanted to think about it.

That, of course, gets him spitting chips.

You told Stirling Seagrave you'd think about it? You, Garvey Quinn, actually told Stirling Seagrave you'd think about it?

I don't know why some people need to repeat everything, even though it's obvious you heard them the first time.

Yeah. I, Garvey Quinn, actually told Stirling Seagrave I'd think about it. I told Stirling Seagrave I'd think about it, OK?

Not OK. Don't you think you have some responsibility to other people as well as yourself?

This is what I mean about people putting pressure on me. It's times like this I wonder if I should have gone for that plumber's apprenticeship Dad had lined up. Those guys make as much as I do and nobody raves at them about responsibility. A job is a job.

Do you know how hard I had to push to get Seagrave's people to even mention your name to him? Every actor in Australia's queuing up for this part, I mean guys who can really act. Do you think Seagrave would be offering the role to an out of work soapie actor if I hadn't broken my balls?

This is once in a lifetime stuff. If you turn this down, you'll never work again – nobody else would want to hire somebody that stupid.

It's not hard to understand why Stuie's so pissed off, because opportunities like this one wouldn't come across his desk all that often. He doesn't have many clients, and most of them are pretty much like me, not a lot of training behind us, in the business because someone liked the look of you when you were eighteen or so and gave you a walk-on in *Home and Away* or *Neighbours*, and it just rolled on from there. Of course people get you to do workshops and such, and I can even croak out a song or two, which Stuie says could be useful if something like *Jesus Christ Superstar* or the *Rocky Horror Show* comes up while you're hot. Basically if people know you're from TV they'll want to see you do other stuff, so be prepared to grab it while it's going, Stuie says.

So I suppose I can see his point. Though it seems to me that blowing out your body with junk food till you look like my Auntie Janice is a bit different from prancing round in lace panties in *Rocky Horror*.

I haven't said I won't do it, I tell him. But Stuie isn't interested in what I've got to say.

Do you know how many guys like you there are around the place, known only for one role in something like *Medical Emergency*? Known, that is, until next season when the next lot of good looking young hunks come along in shows that are equally forgettable? Let me tell you, this morning when I stopped to put petrol in my car the guy at the till said, how you going, Stuie, like he knew me. Afterwards I realised he did, because five years ago he was the star of another dimwitted hospital drama and he was one of my clients. A couple of years after the show folded he changed agents because he said I wasn't getting him enough work, I was holding back his career. Do you want to end up like him, Garvey?

What, change agents?

Working in a service station, you dork.

People seem to be doing this a lot to me at the moment, jumping down my throat because I don't pick up exactly the right sense of what they're saying, same as Seagrave did yesterday. By this stage I feel like just saying yes to the job just to get everybody off my back.

Can't you just phone him up and say, fine, I'll do it?

I can see Stuie reaching for the phone, but he's too wound up to let me off this easily.

I'll level with you, Garvey. The only reason Seagrave's people even considered putting your name forward to the great man wasn't because you can act. It was because you can swim.

★ ★ ★

Once something's signed and sealed I'm pretty good at just accepting that that's the way things are and getting on with the job. Why worry and worry about something that's out of your control? And the one bright spot I can see on the horizon as I head home after talking to Stuie is that Madeleine's going to be so pleased with what I've done she'll be all over me. At last I'll be a real actor, and what could turn her on more than that?

I've already left a message on the machine telling her I'm in the movie, and when I arrive home I see her car outside, so she must know by now, and I walk in the front door expecting her to leap onto me. What I find instead is Madeleine sprawled out on the sofa in a washed-out baggy old tracksuit, looking like something the cat dragged in, her hair all greasy and knotted and sticking out all over the place. She's had it cut just a couple of days ago in a sort of bob that really suits her thin, delicate face, but now it's like a bird's nest. Her faced is drained of colour, except under her eyes, where there are big half circles of browny purple. She seems to hardly even recognise me as I walk over and bend down to kiss her.

So, what do you think? I ask her.

She blinks at me, as if she's only just taking in who I am. Sorry, what?

The role. The movie. Stirling Seagrave. I'm in.

Oh, yes, right, she tells me. Sorry, I'm still in character.

I should have remembered. She's been doing this low-budget movie where she plays a girl from some ritzy family who just won't fit in, so they pack her off to one psychiatric hospital after another trying to cure her, and of course she ends up as a complete suicidal wreck. Today they were shooting the scenes where she's given electric shock therapy, and I should have realised it would take its toll. About all I can think of to do is make a bit of small talk.

Your hair's looking wild, I tell her.

This seems to remind her a bit more of who and where she is. She props herself up a bit and runs her fingers through her hair, pulling at a few of the tangles, then looking at some sort of gunk on her fingertips.

Oh, yes, sorry, she says. I was going to wash it before you got home but I just didn't have the energy. When they did the shock scenes they put this gel on my scalp so the electrodes would stay on properly. Otherwise the current wouldn't go through.

I ask, they used real electricity on you?

Yes. The director thought that when I was doing all that twitching and convulsing on the bed, it would be good if I had something to react to. Not a big shock, just a little bit of a buzz.

Shit.

She sits up more, now, and at last gives me a little smile.

So, that's great about the movie, she tells me.

Yeah, I say. What a challenge, eh? Not only working with Stirling Seagrave, but having to do that to my body.

She looks at me blankly again.

What?

Didn't you realise? To play Bryan Mars as he was at the end, I've got to get really fat, like he was. Stirling Seagrave says you can't fake a thing like that, it has to be absolutely real.

I see her looking me up and down, as if she's assessing my body, and she's got a worried look. It's a while before she says anything.

Well, Garvey, in our business, truth is all that matters, isn't it?, whatever the sacrifice we have to make.

I've had enough of that sort of talk for one day, and I think I deserve some sort of reward for what I've allowed myself to do. I sit down and give Madeleine a kiss and a hug.

What a day, I say. Want to go out to dinner, or shall we get something in and just lie around? I think this calls for some champagne.

It's like she's hardly even heard me. Suddenly she breaks free of my arms and looks at her watch.

Oh God, I'm late for rehearsal!

What rehearsal?

I said I'd do this play, she tells me, it came up at the last minute, it's this interesting project they're doing down at Wooden Leg.

Any play that's called a project has got to be a bit of a

worry, and I can't understand why she'd do this to herself. Or to me.

But you're doing a movie.

I'm just having to fit rehearsals in when I can. And they're being very flexible.

Great. That's really good of them.

She's off and running, grabbing her car keys on the way to the door. She turns back to me as she's stepping outside.

Fantastic about the part, Garvey. This could be the making of you as an actor.

Then she's gone, so I have to celebrate alone, if that's what I'm doing. I get a can of beer from the fridge and turn on the TV, looking for something light and stupid, a comedy, something to distract me, but all I get is sports news and a re-run of *Medical Emergency*.

★ ★ ★

Within days they got me into the pool. It all seemed a bit unnecessary, the training regime they were putting me through. I mean, looking like an Olympic swimmer is one thing, but there was no need for me to actually be capable of winning a gold medal. But what Seagrave wanted, apparently, was for me not to just look like a swimmer, but to actually feel like one. In other words, totally shagged out most of the time.

I was put into training with a squad run by Arthur Snow, who'd been Bryan Mars's coach in his heyday. He was renowned for being so tough that most swimmers who started with him usually left after a few months and went to somebody softer. Supposedly Bryan Mars was the only swimmer who could ever keep up with Arthur Snow's training schedule. The legend was that Mars did everything Snow asked of him and then turned round and asked for more because he thought he wasn't being pushed hard enough. That was in the golden years, before it all turned sour and Snow kicked him out of the squad.

Snow's going to be portrayed in the movie too, of course, played by Duncan Young, one of the senior actors in the profession, one of those gnarly old drunks who's in practically everything.

So, for the sake of realism, every morning at five o'clock I turn up at the Aquatic Centre and just swim and swim and swim, up and down for two hours like some sort of robot, only stopping when I hear Arthur Snow shouting at me. Which is something he does a lot.

You! Shit-for-brains! What do you think you're doing? Do you call yourself a swimmer?

Er, no, I'm an actor.

I look up from the pool at Arthur Snow. Though he never gets in the water, when the sun comes out he always strips down to nothing but a tight little pair of Speedos, which don't go well with the big gut that hangs over them. Snow's one of those old guys who's spent most of his life in the sun, burnt almost black and wrinkled up everywhere like a prune. He seems to spend a lot of time hitching up his balls.

Listen Sonny Jim, when you're in this pool, with me coaching you, either you're a swimmer or you can piss off right now. Don't talk to me about acting.

Sorry.

You're not even breathing, do you realise that?

To me this seems a bit of an exaggeration. I must have been up and down that pool thirty times in this session, and I know enough about the human body to figure out that if I really wasn't breathing I'd be dead by now.

Wasn't I?

Garvey Quinn

You're breathing like you're sucking a milkshake up through a straw. Don't you realise, your lungs are your engine, and when you breathe it's got to be like your mouth is a turbocharger, blasting the fuel in. Come on, get it right, one two three four breathe. One two three four breathe.

So I go one two three four breathe, one two three four breathe, up and down the pool for what seems like forever, but which in reality was probably only about four laps. At the end, I feel like I must have done really well, I'm gasping for breath, slumped back against the side of the pool, my head spinning, starting to forget where I am and what's going on. Until I hear Arthur Snow.

That was piss poor. I'm used to working with champions. Why am I wasting my time on the likes of you?

Probably the answer is that the producers have paid him heaps of money to work with the likes of me, plus it gets him back in the limelight, where he hasn't been for quite a while. But I'm too exhausted to answer, and my stare back at him must confirm everything he thinks about me. His hand goes down to fiddle with his balls again.

You just couldn't give a fuck, could you Sonny Jim?

I watch him stamp off, for about the third time today, with one of Seagrave's minions running after him. And I know that he's absolutely right. I couldn't give a fuck about this, most of the time anyway, so it's no wonder that's how I look. I'm not sure I'd want to give a fuck about this kind of thing. It's one thing to do ten or twenty laps on a sunny day with a couple of mates around and the prospect of a beer afterwards, but this, the serious stuff, most of all it's just dead boring, up and down the pool with nothing to think about but what's inside your head. It makes me wonder. Apart from all the other stuff, did Bryan Mars just go a bit crazy from too much swimming? And am I going to go crazy too?

It also stuffs around the rest of your life. Knowing that even when you wake up, or especially when you wake up, you'll have this dead tired feeling, every muscle in your body sort of aching slightly. And no prospect of it getting any better, because after you've done your morning session, you go home and have lunch, put your head down for a minute, and then suddenly it's time to get up again and do the afternoon session. Which Arthur Snow believes should always be tougher than the morning one, to give you a feeling of progression. What amazes me most is that there are people doing this for year after year, not like me, who knows it'll be all over in a few months, but kids of twelve who are facing what must look like half a lifetime of doing nothing but this. All I can say is the pay-off would have to be pretty big. To put yourself through this you'd want to collect absolutely everything that was going at the end of it, all the medals and the glory and the millions from the breakfast food endorsements, and maybe that's the key to the Bryan Mars character, that in the end it wasn't worth it. I don't know.

The toll on your personal life, that's the big thing. Three weeks into the training, I have to go straight from the pool to this theatre in the inner city called the Wooden Leg, in an old prosthetics factory, for the opening night of that play Madeleine's in. She's been working hard too, but training's been knocking me around so much I haven't really been able to get the gist of what she's doing. About all I'm aware of is she keeps asking me about whether her bum's all right, and all I can say is, yeah, your bum looks great. Which is true.

I've had a quick shower, but I just can't get this chlorine smell out of my nose, and I wonder if other people can smell it on me too. It feels like I'm saturated with the stuff. Not that it should surprise anybody, everybody in the business knows by now that I'm the lucky guy who's scored the lead role in Stirling Seagrave's movie about Bryan Mars. It's getting heaps of media coverage, and I even made it onto *Sports World* last Sunday, after a crew came out and filmed me at training. As I walk in, feeling exhausted right into my bones, I get congratulations right and left, and slaps on the back, because half the audience seem to be actors too, and I know that underneath all the generosity they're thinking, why him? Which is a question I've started to ask myself quite a bit too.

Stuie Fengler's there. He's Madeleine's agent too, and I sit with him. When he asks me how I am, I tell him straight that I'm completely fucked, but he tries to reassure me that it's all worth it. The industry buzz about *Fish Out of Water* is huge, he tells me, they're already talking about American distribution deals, the whole thing. I'm about to ask him whether there's anything in my contract about that, because after all I'm the bloke doing all the hard work, but then the lights go down, I mean not just down, but completely pitch black, and it stays that way for about two minutes, and then this one little spotlight comes on, and it lights up a bare bum in the middle of the stage. Madeleine's bare bum – I recognise it right away, even with the state I'm in, only half awake.

I don't get to a lot of plays, except for the stuff Madeleine's in, and I've never really wanted to be in one, somehow I just can't see the point, doing the same thing night after night after night, so maybe I'm not the best person to judge. But I have to say, apart from the sight of Madeleine's bum, this show wasn't great. It's supposed to be based on something from the classics, Greek or Norwegian or whatever, but apparently the director more or less made it up in rehearsal, so Madeleine was getting back to the flat each night not knowing whether she was coming or going, and yet at the same time saying, there's an extraordinary journey of exploration happening here. At least that's one thing you can say for Stirling Seagrave, he wouldn't have a bar of that sort of journey of exploration crap, though I wouldn't be surprised if he asks me to bare my bum.

I stay with the story as far as the part where the main bloke comes back from some war to find that his wife and his son have shacked up together and don't know that they're related. When you describe it like that, it sounds interesting, like a Tasmanian joke, but they just seem to talk on and on and on, and the way I'm feeling after all the swimming, I just can't stop myself nodding off. At one stage I feel Stuie Fengler elbow me to try to wake me up, but it's a losing battle, I'm so drowsy, and pretty soon I'm out to it. In retrospect, it's a pity I was sitting in the front row, but it's not like I went to sleep on purpose.

Afterwards in the bar, people are acting strangely towards me. I get sniggers from people who'd been sitting nearby. From the actors in the play, I get glares. One of them, Austin Irwin, once did a guest spot on *Medical Emergency* and moaned the whole time about the script and the director and the coffee and everything else you could think of. I've always thought he was up himself, and I don't think he's much of an actor either, but he's come out into the bar like he's making a grand entrance on Oscar night, expecting everyone to kiss his arse. He gets lots of hugs and kisses and, oh, Austin, you were fantastic, though not from me. I'm doing my best to keep right out of his way, and wondering why Madeleine's taking so long to come out of the dressing room. I can't keep dodging Austin, though, and in the end he corners me up against the bar.

Got your mind on higher things, have you Garvey? he says, and I haven't got a clue what he means.

Just a bit tired from all the training they're making me do for the movie, I explain. I know people like him think I'm too thick to understand the sort of stuff they do in theatres like this, so I at least want him to know there's a legitimate reason.

Oh yes, of course, your big role in *Wet Dream*.

What?

That's what they're calling it around the industry. Anyway, congratulations on getting it. I promise when I go and see it I'll try not to snore.

Moments after Austin slips away, Madeleine at last comes out of the dressing rooms, and I can see right away she's as mad as hell.

You were like a buzz saw. It was so embarrassing.

Sorry, it's all the training.

Just tell me one thing. Was I all right?

You never looked better. Especially your …

After that she doesn't speak to me for the rest of the night, and nobody else does much either, so I just sit in a corner nursing a light beer, and even that's more than I'm supposed to have, now that I'm in training. I have this new feeling of being sort of different, above it all, not part of the same world as everybody else, and I wonder if that's how Bryan Mars felt too. Could that have been the seed of his downfall? Then, the funny thing is, as I'm drifting off into more thoughts about Bryan Mars and what made him tick, I look up for a moment just as this group of people are heading out the door into the night, and I'm sure, in the middle of them, I see Stirling Seagrave. I half get up, thinking I should run after him and have a word, but I don't carry it through, partly because my legs don't seem to want to move that fast, and partly because I'm thinking, isn't that a strange way to behave? To cast you in the lead role in his movie, but then when he turns up at the same play as you, to not even bother coming over to say hello? To be honest, that sort of thing worries me, because it's not how I was taught to behave.

When Madeleine does talk to me again, it's because she wants to go on somewhere with the cast, some club with a door nazi, and naturally I'm invited, I'm not that much on the outer, but I just haven't got it in me. In the old days I would have been into that like a rat up a drainpipe, but it's nearly midnight and I'm aware that in five hours I have to get up and head for the pool, with God knows how many laps ahead of me. Strangely, even though I'm not enjoying doing all this swimming, I just can't stop imagining myself doing it, feel my arm coming over and pulling through the water, one two three four breathe, Bryan Mars's stroke exactly, one two three four breathe, even when people are talking to me, that's what I'm thinking about, one two three four breathe, it seems to take over everything, no reason left to worry, no reason to think. So I have to tell them, thanks but no thanks, and I even find myself talking like an athlete, sorry, if I don't hit the sack soon I'll be ratshit at training tomorrow. Austin Irwin's there, smirking away.

Really living the part, aren't you, Garvey. The way he says this pisses me off, because it makes me sound like some method wanker. All I am is an actor doing a job.

Back at the flat, I wake up from a dream which, surprisingly, is about swimming. I'm pounding up and down the pool but it's just getting emptier and emptier and somehow I have to finish my laps before it runs out of water completely, and I'm not going to make it, and I'm desperate about it, and then there's the relief of waking up, and I see Madeleine sitting next to me on the bed, stretching her arms behind her as she takes off her bra. Even in my hazy state I enjoy watching her do this as much as ever, and I look at the clock to see whether there's enough of the night left to squeeze in a quick one and still get a bit more shut-eye before training. There is, just, but there's also just enough light in the room to be able to see the expression on Madeleine's face, and it's obvious she's not in the mood.

Garvey, there's something I have to tell you, she says to me.

I've had a couple of other girlfriends say this to me in the past, and it always sends a chill up my spine, like they're just about to lower the boom. I wonder, is she going to tell me she's having it off with Austin Irwin, or is she pregnant, like my brother Dean's girlfriend hit him with, or what?

What?

I'm in the movie too.

I'm not quite awake enough to think this through.

What movie?

Even in this light, I can see how she's looking at me, the way lots of people seem to when I don't get the idea right away.

The same movie you're in, of course. What other movie would I be talking about?

Now I do get the idea.

Since when?

Since last night, at the play.

Is that why Stirling Seagrave was there?

I don't know why he was there, but he offered me the part. I'm playing your girlfriend.

Vicki Michaels? The one who picks up three gold medals while poor Bryan's disgracing himself, and leaves him for a Swedish pole vaulter?

The very same. So, are you pleased for me?

Well, yeah, of course I am. Yeah, that's great.

I am pleased. I'm always glad to see Madeleine get a break, she deserves it, the way she works so hard and thinks so much, it's more than I could do, I just wait for it all to happen. Madeleine deserves all the success in the world. But I'm really spooked by the sneaky way Stirling Seagrave's gone about this, and I want to know more. Madeleine's great, but there are heaps of other good actresses out there, so why choose the one who lives with the leading man? I ask her the only question I can think of, to try to figure out what it is that Seagrave wants to get from Madeleine, that nobody else could give.

Did Seagrave make any comment about your performance?

He said my bum was great.

What worries me about this development is what it's going to do to our life together. Unlike Madeleine, I never like to bring my work home with me. Sure I bring the script home and put in an hour or so memorising the lines, but there usually aren't too many of them, and they're not all that difficult to say. The rest of the time, until I roll up to the studio in the morning, I find other things to think about. Real things, like how good my WRX Impreza feels when the turbo kicks in.

With Madeleine though, it's different. Any time she's been in a play, I've had weeks of her 'inhabiting the part', as she calls it. During the rehearsal phase, she'll pace around the flat all night going over and over the same lines till they just stop meaning anything, till it all just sounds like gibberish. I remember when she was graduating from drama school and they were doing some play about a tram, and she just went over and over this one line, something about the kindness of strangers, and it got to the stage where I was thinking if she says that one more time I'll just go stark raving bonkers.

But even worse is all the psychological stuff, what is my character feeling now, what is the action I'm performing now, what is the subtext of that action, when my character says, open the door, in what imperceptible but important way does that change my character's relationship with the other characters, and what does that opening of that door actually symbolise, what's really at stake here? All of this, on and on for weeks.

Ordinarily I'd say, fine, that's what she does, she thinks it's part of her job, and if it makes her feel secure, well, what's the harm? But this time, because we're both in the same thing, I've got no choice but to get involved in it too, her bouncing lines off me, what does this line really mean?, what am I really doing here?, questions questions questions. Short of having a row about it, though, there's nothing I can do except cop it sweet.

One person who isn't going to cop it sweet, though, is my dad, and when we go and visit him on his birthday, my biggest worry is that she'll talk acting the whole time. My dad has enough trouble putting up with me being an actor anyway, after all he did to set up that plumber's apprenticeship with his mate, and he only sort of accepts it because I've been on early evening TV and there's nothing arty-farty about it, and I made it onto the cover of *TV Week*. The money's OK by him too, especially when I've told him about Mel or Arnie or Tom's salary for the latest thing they're in, but actually talking about acting, no, that just gets right up his nose. Best just to keep clear of that, and I tell Madeleine straight, look, let's have a break from work talk today. After all, it's Dad's birthday, so the day should be about him. Madeleine gives me that look that says nothing's going to stop her doing exactly what she wants to do.

He's your dad. What you do is important to him. What better birthday present could you give him than to show him that you've graduated to becoming a real actor tackling a complex dramatic role, instead of being just some airhead in a soapie?

Airhead? I didn't know you thought being in the soaps made me an airhead.

You know what I mean, Garvey. It was a way into the profession, and sometimes it exposed you to people who had their sights set on higher things. But it was hardly something you could be proud of artistically, was it? Churning out pulp for people who couldn't care what they were watching. It didn't exactly nourish your creative spirit.

This is dangerous stuff, considering what my mum said about nourishing her creative spirit when she was telling Dad she was leaving him, but we're on the doorstep with the doorbell ringing, and it's too late to rein things in now. Dad pulls the door open and shuffles back from it, wearing shorts, thongs and a singlet, just like I expected, and I have to admit, it makes sense dressing like that on a hot day if you're not going out, and I'd do it myself if Madeleine hadn't made such a fuss and thrown my thongs away. Madeleine gives Dad a big hug and a kiss for his birthday, but he's such an unemotional guy he doesn't seem to know what to make of it, and just grunts, how you going, Maddy? He's got the cricket going on TV. It's the second Test with England on the ropes and the crowd howling for blood, and Dad's right into it too, hardly even looking away when we hand over his present, which is a kind of Hawaiian-looking shirt that Madeleine chose, nothing to do with me because I know how much he likes his singlet.

Yeah, that's real beaut, is all he says, but I know he's not even going to take the plastic wrapper off, it'll just go up on top of the wardrobe alongside whatever it was we got him last birthday and Christmas, more shirts probably. He's never liked people making a fuss about things, all that family celebration stuff, and since he's been on his own he's really shut up shop. In a way I think he blames me for what happened, and maybe Madeleine even more so, kind of guilt by association. Looking at it reasonably, you can't blame us for inviting Mum along to that play that Madeleine was in, the one about the giant cockroach, and nor can you blame us for her meeting Howie, the lighting designer, in the foyer afterwards. And once people meet up and find they like each other, once the chemistry takes over, what can you do?

That was LBW for sure, you dickhead, Dad's shouting, at the TV rather than us. Look at the way the ball's moving around, they'll be lucky to reach a hundred even with umpiring like that. Then a wicket does fall, and after the shouting, Dad gets up because he knows there's a long ad break coming up, he gets up and goes to the fridge. He comes back with a bottle of Reschs and a couple of glasses, and starts pouring without even asking us if we want any. Just remembered my manners, he says. But Madeleine pulls her glass away and gestures at him to stop filling mine.

No thanks Mr Quinn. We've got training in two hours. Do you have something soft?

Training? You?

Dad's looking suspiciously at us, and I'm not too keen on what's happening either. But Madeleine really does look like somebody in training, perched on the edge of her chair bolt upright in her shorts and her tight silky singlet, the whole of her lungs seeming to swell up with each breath.

Come on, it's Dad's birthday, just one won't hurt.

Are you serious about this part or not, Garvey?

The new Pom batsman gets out first ball, middle stump sent cartwheeling, so Dad's attention's back with us for a while, and Madeleine goes for it, in just the way I was hoping she wouldn't.

Sometimes great art takes real sacrifice, she tells him. We're not just pretending to be these famous swimmers we're playing. We're actually being them.

They can fake just about anything in the movies now, can't they, with computers and stuff, nobody looks at it and thinks it's bloody true.

Of course, that really gets Madeleine going.

Ah, but that's where you're wrong, Mr Quinn –

For Christ's sake call me Ken!

Where you're wrong Ken, is thinking that the truth doesn't matter any more. If the actor isn't giving a truthful performance, an audience can tell. When the audience sees an actor up there on the screen performing in a scene where Bryan Mars pushes himself in training to levels of pain never before experienced by anyone, they have to feel that pain with him. If the actor doesn't feel it, the audience certainly won't. And when he was in training, Bryan Mars would not allow himself just one little drink, even on his father's birthday.

He allowed himself quite a few in the end, didn't he?

Yes. And that, too, is a truth that Garvey will have to capture.

Truth?, Dad snaps at her. If this is truth you can keep it. Bryan Mars was a national disgrace. An embarrassment to every Australian. This country gave him the opportunity to be great, and he couldn't handle it. End of story. Who wants to know any more? We heard enough about it at the time, Jesus, did we ever, we had more than enough of the truth, so much truth about that dickhead it was coming out of our bloody ears.

But Madeleine pushes on, listen to yourself Ken. Listen to how angry you are when you talk about Bryan Mars. Do you know why? Because you're identifying with something universal. Having the world at your feet, and then losing it, through some fatal flaw in your character.

I'm hoping this will all blow over in a minute, now that the drinks trolley's being wheeled off the ground and the new Pom batsman's shuffling over to the wicket with the crowd howling for his blood.

I don't know what you're on about, Dad says, looking at the TV. Jesus, look at this one, he bats like a girl.

Madeleine just won't let go. For example, she says, when your wife left you, wasn't there some moment when you thought, is there some way I could have lived my life differently? Or was all this inevitable?

Dad dribbles his beer when he talks this time, he's looking so pissed off. With me.

What the fuck have you been telling her?

Nothing, Dad. I mean, she was there.

Yeah. She was there. And so were you. And so was my wife. And now I'm here but she isn't. And I don't need to see some movie about the Elvis Presley of swimming to help me see the truth of that.

I pick up the glass Dad didn't finish pouring for me. There's about an inch of beer in it. Madeleine looks at me, and I put it down again. She's not finished.

Ken, do you know why I'm telling you all this? Because I want you to know the importance of the role your son is about to play. And if your son rises to the level of truth the role requires, as I know he will, it'll be a tribute to you. Happy birthday.

Bowled him! Did him like a dinner!

★ ★ ★

The joke's on me. I might agree with Dad when it comes to all this stuff about exploring the symbolic truth of the character, but I've got publicity obligations. I've got to be able to talk about that sort of thing like I believe in it.

This is where I realise how much I'd be missing if Madeleine wasn't around. As soon as I tell her this journalist was on the phone, he's going to interview me tomorrow and he's full of crap about truth, authenticity and responsibility, Madeleine's on the case. She pretends she's the journo, asks me the questions, then coaches me with the answers.

Garvey, you've really been pushing yourself in training. Today at the end you looked so exhausted you could hardly walk. Why do it? I mean is anybody really going to notice when they see the movie?

I'll notice.

Yes, but to most people one swimmer looks pretty much like another once they're in the water. Isn't it the acting they want to see?

Well, I suppose it is, but even so, you have to be able to swim properly, and if –

No no no no no!

Madeleine has come out of character as the journo and gone back to being herself.

For God's sake Garvey, you're not supposed to agree with them. Now think. Why will people notice, why will the amount of training you're doing affect what they see? Come on, you've got to try harder.

It always comes back to that with Madeleine in the end, everything would be all right if people would just try harder. Her old man was head honcho of the local progress association in her home town up on the north coast, so maybe it comes from him.

I try to remember the answer from the session I had with

her last night. I wasn't good at this sort of thing at school, either, remembering the right ideas in the right order, off the cuff. Acting's different because the ideas are already in the lines and you don't have worry about them, the main thing is to remember the words. Then it comes back to me.

But people do notice. And what they notice is truth. A real swimmer swims with every ounce of their being. And for an actor to really get into the soul of the character, they have to know what that's like. And if that truth isn't there, it'll show in everything they do, in and out of the water.

Better. Much better.

Then she's back to being the journo.

But surely film is all about illusion. A good director can make an audience believe anything.

I could happily live without the next bit, but Madeleine thinks it'll do me good.

I'm working with a wonderful director. Stirling Seagrave's just brilliant. But I feel I owe it to him to give him the best possible material to work with, and if that means killing myself in training, well, that's the price you have to pay for art.

Very good, Garvey. Especially about the price of art.

★ ★ ★

BRYAN MARS

First thing when you wake up you think, yes, I am like this. Yes, it is like this. You think, what's going to happen today? You realise. Same as yesterday. Same as the day before and the day before. Nothing. Eating. TV. Your mum going down to the shops for another truckload of food for you. More eating. More TV. Your mum saying, a walk would do you good, Bryan, a bit of fresh air. You walk out the back so no one can see you. If you can call it walking. Does a jelly walk? You step out of the air-conditioning and wobble half-way down the backyard. The tropical heat of Darwin hits you like a slap with a steamy wet towel. You give up, you walk back inside, you lie down, take the weight off your feet. You've got a lot of weight to take off your feet. They're big, fat feet. They were always big, but now they're big and fat. Hard to believe the same feet used to propel you through the water like you had an outboard motor strapped on. You lie down with a magazine. Sort that used to have you in it. TV stars, sports stars, who's getting up who on the sly. You wish you could be interested in something else, something higher than this, good books or something, but your mind just can't hold onto those, because the only story is your own, it just won't let you go long enough to take in anything else except these shorts bites. You look at the pictures, half a page here, half a page there, read the headlines and not much more, millionaire horse trainer's battle with the bottle, TV weathergirl gets bigger boobs, Gaddafi's thugs stole my kidney. It's the same as you eat, you could never sit down for a full meal, you just take in a bit here and bit there, all the time, lots of small bits of junk to somehow fill the hole. You see your mum drive back with the big super family size tub of Kentucky Fried, and the worst thing is you feel excited, though it's the same as this morning, and you think, this'll take you two hours to eat, which at least is two hours that's taken care of. You see your mum's got the new *TV Week* as well, which you're pleased about, because you've read last week's from cover to cover and back again ten times, along with all the other junk, *Who* and *Real Life* and *People* and all the rest of the stuff, and you grab at the *TV Week* as soon as your mum comes in only she pulls it away because she wants to show you something. She holds it up so you can see the cover and there's this actor there, this Garvey Quinn who used to be on *Medical Emergency*, that show they killed, it was never one of your favourites but at least it was something to watch. Your mum says to you, in this excited voice you hardly ever hear from her these days, look son, I told you they'd recognise your true greatness one day, they're going to make a movie about your life, and they've got that lovely Garvey Quinn who used to play Doctor Simon Dennis in *Medical Emergency*, he's so handsome, nearly as handsome as you. You see your mum getting red in the face she's so happy about this, Bryan, darling, this could be a whole new beginning for you. But you don't want a new beginning, that's the last thing you want, you just want to keep it all away from you until one day you feel like none of it ever happened. But a moment later you're thinking, the bastards, how dare they make a movie of your life without asking your permission? But then you remember, everybody thinks you're dead, which is exactly what you wanted them to think. But Garvey Quinn? You think, shit, couldn't they even have bothered hiring someone who could act?

Now you find that everywhere you look, there's you. Your mum's buying every magazine and newspaper she can find, not just the usual ones, but everything that's going, just like she used to when you were famous. Now you're famous again, you just have to flip over a page of *Woman's Day* or *Aussie Post* or any of them, and there's all the old photos of you, you ploughing through the water, breaking your first world record, you with Mum, you training with the squad, Arthur Snow shouting at you and waving his stopwatch, you in a dinner suit looking pleased with yourself, Sportsman of the Year, you holding hands with Vicki at your birthday party, another one of you and her cuddling up in the pool, it's like the whole world owns your family photo album. You want to look away, why would you want to see this stuff again? But your mum turns the page, there's more, there's you, the hero, getting your bravery medal after the rescue, and at the aquarium standing next to a shark said to be virtually identical to the one you punched out. And you being driven around in Alexander Morton's Rolls-Royce, and then the nightclub scenes, the punch-up, and look at that little roll of fat under the chin, they've even drawn an arrow on the picture just in case anyone's so stupid they can't spot it for themselves. Then fatso at the pool, your anguished face when you've missed the squad, then there you are even bigger in your Channel 7 blazer, holding a microphone out trying to interview someone you would have beaten by half the length of the pool just a few months before, you can't even remember his name he was that inconsequential, and probably no one else remembers him either, but they remember you, and with all this going on, they're not going to forget now, how

StUffED

many more years is it going to be before it all fades away?

Your mum's smiling, like she's still proud of you, she's saying, you're still respected out there son, and when you decide to make your comeback, when you give yourself back to the world they'll welcome you with open arms, you just had a few setbacks, but once a champion always a champion, this will probably be a whole new beginning for you and on and on and on, until you leave the room. You go out to the kitchen to get yourself the last beer in the fridge, and on the way back through the house you turn on the TV for some distraction. You find a current affairs program, you'd think that'd be safe, but no, there you are, who else could that be in the pool but you, with that style. But now they're showing this Garvey Quinn bloke, the actor who's going to be impersonating you, they've got him training with Arthur Snow, and Arthur's shouting at him the way he used to shout at you, and Garvey Quinn's even got his hair exactly the way you used to have yours, must have tracked down that hairdresser. You listen, don't want to, but you can't help it, to this actor talking about authenticity and truth and all the rest of it, how he couldn't play you without putting himself through what you went through. When you see him swim, in spite of all the bullshit, he's hopeless, he wouldn't have come within a mile of making the Olympic team, and with that and not being able to act either, you can tell this movie about your life is going to be nothing short of a travesty. Then when the director comes on, this Stirling Seagrave, who's one of those people you hate from the moment you set eyes on him, you hear him saying that the story of Bryan Mars is the quintessential story of our times, it captures the spirit of the age, there's an essential symbolic truth about how his triumph turned to tragedy. That's when you get up, you finished that beer in a couple of gulps, and you need more.

You don't dare ask your mum to go out again, she'd be happy to, she always is, but you know that as well as coming back with a slab, she'd have a couple more magazines with her, more stories about you.

So you go out yourself, first time in God knows how long. You can't quite believe you're doing it, taking this chance of being recognised, but you walk out into the heat, not as bad as before, but the way you are, carrying so much flesh around with you, it's hard going, you're puffing and groaning with every step. You've got the biggest, baggiest clothes your mum could find in the Big Men's Shop, and then she let them out by another metre or so, but even so, everything's still tight around your bum and your crotch and across your gut and under the arms; you can feel the sweat pouring through the cloth. You keep out of the streetlights because you know what a sight you must be, but when you get to the shopping centre nothing's open but the bottle shop and the mini-market. All the lights are full on, floodlights on account of the street crime, and there's nothing for it but to just let yourself be seen, just take whatever happens to you now, and somehow it doesn't seem to matter that much anymore, what more can they do?

Bloke at the counter hardly looks up at you, he's got the TV on, another current affairs show, and there you are again, you hardly even glance at it as you go by towards the coolroom, but you know instantly that's the last lap of your fifteen hundred metres world record, the third time you broke it, one month before you accepted the invite to go out on Alexander Morton's boat. You see yourself reflected in the glass of the coolroom door, and you wonder if you swelled up even bigger walking through the heat, because you're a balloon now, a blimp, how could anybody look at you anymore and recognise you as that guy in the pool? Even your face has changed, it looks like it's made of pizza dough, and with all the hair and the beard, there's nothing of the old Bryan Mars left for anyone to recognise.

You pick up your carton of VB and you walk back towards the counter, wondering if you should have bought two. Somehow you're calm, first time out in years and you're going to get away with it, you just dig the money out of your pocket and drop it on the counter, but he's staring at you from under the rim of his cowboy hat. You're him, he's saying to you, you're him, you're Bryan Mars! You don't even wait for your change, you're owed a couple of dollars but it doesn't matter, you've already got the slab over your shoulder, so you run with it as best you can, puffing and blowing, you barge the doors open, but there's three guys and a woman all coming in at once and the shopkeeper's behind you, he's calling out, it's Bryan Mars, it's Bryan Mars. You drop the slab and hear the stubbies smash, you try running faster but the insides of your thighs are rubbing together so hard the friction slows you down, and the voices are closing in on you, it's Bryan Mars, it's Bryan Mars, Bryan Mars is still alive!

★ ★ ★

GarVEY QUiNN

Stirling Seagrave turns out to be a pig to work with, which doesn't surprise me one bit. Nothing I do is ever good enough. In his eyes I'm not an actor's arsehole, and he lets everybody know this at the top of his voice as often as he possibly can. There's this one particular scene where Bryan Mars has a blow-up with Arthur Snow. Arthur wants him to miss the Commonwealth Games so he doesn't have to taper off his training, and instead go for the world record a few months later. But Bryan says, no, he can't let his country down, because even though the Commonwealth games might be a Mickey Mouse event these days by international standards, Mr and Mrs Average back home in the suburbs still think it's important, and so do the kids who look up to him. I can't believe Bryan Mars ever said any of this crap, but it's what's in the script, and the real Arthur Snow's technical adviser on the movie and he's given it the OK, so I'm stuck with it.

In this scene, Arthur, played by Duncan Young, does his block at Bryan. Duncan Young doesn't look anything like the real Arthur Snow, and he certainly never strips down to his Speedos, thank Christ, instead staying in one of those old-fashioned clingy blue nylon tracksuits with the white stripes. I see the make-up girls trying to put tan on his face, but he still looks exactly like what he is: a puffy pink-skinned bloke who lives in a pub.

Arthur tells Bryan, that's it, as far as he's concerned, either he does what he's told or he can find a new coach, and let's see how far he gets with anybody else. There's all this stuff about how you'd have been nothing without me, I've made sacrifices for you, Bryan, more than you could ever understand, son, because I believe in you, but there's one thing I expect more than anything else and that's loyalty, and I don't care who you are or how much talent you've got, that's my bottom line.

And then Bryan Mars, that's me, has to say, listen, Arthur, nobody could have done more for me than you did, I owe you the world, but I also owe the people out there something, and this time I'm going to be swimming for them. I'll worry about the world record another time.

And at that point, I have to sling my towel over my shoulder and start walking away, and then Arthur has to say, you leave it too late, you might never get the world record. And I turn back to him and I say, I could break the world record now, and Arthur says, bullshit. So I grab a stopwatch, shove it in his hands and say, watch me, and I dive in. And then there, in the almost deserted pool, Arthur watches open mouthed as I churn up and down and cut four seconds off the record, unofficially of course, without anybody to push me. Then of course, later on in the story, after I've won gold in the Commonwealth Games and broken the world record doing it, I'm being challenged by this new hot swimmer from Romania, and suddenly I need a coach again and I go crawling back to Arthur, and we have this tearful reunion.

In this scene, the break-up, and setting the unofficial world record, you wouldn't have thought there was that much to do. It's stuff pretty much like I'd done dozens of times on *Medical Emergency*. The standard blow-up scene, Doctor, I'm giving you an ultimatum, if you don't do what I'm telling you to do you're finished in the medical profession, and then I say, I'm sorry, I have to do what my conscience tells me, we're talking about a patient's life here, etc, etc, well, I could do that stuff in my sleep. Stirling Seagrave, though, wants me to mumble the words out through my teeth, with all these pauses and staring off into the water and fiddling with my cossie, which is hard to do without actually touching your knob. If you did the whole movie like that it'd be five hours long, and nobody would watch it. But he's the director, so I do my best which, like I said, is never good enough. I say, I could break the world record now, and to me, that's the sort of line you'd shout, you're, like, making a big, defiant statement, something you want to get over with fast. Even I know that much about human behaviour. But instead, after Arthur says, you might never get the world record, Seagrave wants me to stare at the far end of the pool for what seems like forever, as if I'm measuring the distance, then hitch up my Speedos, then look back at Arthur, bite my lip, look at the pool again, then back to Arthur for a long stare into his eyes, and only then say, I could break the world record now. And we do it dozens of times, and either I don't stare long enough at the end of the pool, or I'm looking up too high, or I forget to fiddle with my swimmers, or I bite my top lip instead of my bottom lip, or I don't look into Arthur's eyes for long enough. It seems like I can get most of them right, but never all of them at once.

Finally, on the umpteenth run at it, I seem to have got it all together, the stare, the fiddle, the look back, the lip biting, the look away, the look back, all pretty near perfect, but then I blow the line. A couple of times I've said I could beat the world record, when I'm supposed to say break, so I've kept reminding myself, the word starts b-r-e, b-r-e, b-r-e, but this time, with everything else going right I say, I could breast the world record, and everybody falls about laughing, everybody except Seagrave, who throws his script on the ground.

To me all this seems a bit unfair. It's not easy acting and remembering lines at the same time, and the worse I get, the ruder Seagrave is, and the more nervous I get, so what do they expect to happen? Duncan Young isn't a help either, playing Arthur, he seems to be doing it on automatic pilot, ducking off for a little nip from his flask every couple of takes, and smiling all the time like he thinks the whole thing's a joke. But then when the camera rolls, there he is, exactly like the last time, and I'm getting so sick of hearing that growly voice, you might never get the world record, somehow next time through it provokes me into shouting the line back at him, I could break the world record right now, at the top of my voice, without any of the pauses and the mucking about with my cossie and staring.

Of course, this really sets Seagrave off, he's got this loud-hailer that he uses when he wants to talk to anyone, like his voice wasn't loud enough already, and he yells into it, are you deliberately trying to sabotage this picture or are you just a complete fucking moron? Now I happen to take a certain pride in doing a job properly. I don't give a flying fuck about art but I believe in doing the job and there's no way I'd ever sabotage something I was working on, no matter how much of a prick the director might be.

What do you reckon? I'm a complete fucking moron, I say.

This gets Seagrave looking so angry that I think he's about to fire me, and to be honest, the way things have been going I couldn't really care if he did.

Yeah, you are a moron, aren't you, and what's more you take a pride in it, don't you, you actually admit to being one, you must think it's funny or something.

I can't stand it when I say something as a kind of a joke, or just for the sake of arguing, and someone like Seagrave acts like I really meant it, and I'm about to say, listen, of course I don't actually think I'm a moron, what sort of idiot would publicly admit to that, but just as I'm about to open my mouth I see some sort of kerfuffle going on over near the pool entrance, and one of those production assistant girls who always seem to be wandering around holding bits of paper comes charging through security and straight up to Seagrave, who looks like he's now about to chew her out for interrupting things, but he doesn't have time before she blurts out, they've found Bryan Mars! Bryan Mars is still alive!

★ ★ ★

Next morning I get a message that filming's been suspended until further notice, which is probably a good thing. If we'd gone on much longer I'd probably have punched Seagrave out, the way I've been practising on the polypropylene shark. Seagrave won't give me or anyone else a reason, and when I phone Stuie to ask him to find out more about what's going on, Stuie isn't that interested.

We have an evolving situation here, he tells me. It's not like some soap opera sausage factory, there's an artist at work, and when you need to know something, I'm sure you'll be told.

I find this hard to deal with, it makes me sort of restless, and about all I can do is pace around the flat. Madeleine goes off early to do a training session, slipping out trying not to wake me, though I stir long enough to get a good look at her stepping into her cossie, the muscles at the tops of her thighs clenching as she lifts up one leg, then the other, to squeeze into the suit. Then, before she pulls up the top part to anchor it round her neck, she has a fiddle with the crotch, probably checking to make sure everything's covered, and when she leans over a bit for a closer look, her boobs don't sag at all, just keep poking straight from her chest. This always makes me hard and I think of pulling her back to bed for a quickie, though I know she won't be into it, she's less and less into it these days, as if she's got some notion that too much sex is bad for the serious athlete. From what I heard, Bryan Mars certainly wasn't averse to getting his end in, no matter how many world records he was breaking.

But with Madeleine gone, and being fobbed of by Stuie like that, I don't quite know what to do with myself, so I try putting the TV on. All I can find are daytime soaps, American stuff, even worse than ours, all big jaws and blow-waves and silicone tits. So I channel hop, hoping I might at least find some interesting ads, or some home shopping, people flogging those funny banana-shaped exercise machines that are supposed to work off your beergut. Then I find some afternoon news, coming in halfway through an item about a woman who cut off her husband's prong and put it in the microwave. When the newsreader comes back, on the wall behind him there's a huge blown-up photograph of Bryan Mars, Mars when he was the golden boy, smiling after breaking a world record, hair as perfect as mine, and the newsreader's saying, there's been a surprise new development in the Bryan Mars situation. After hiding from the media spotlight for the past two days, the controversial former swimming star emerged from his house to be picked up by an unmarked helicopter and whisked away to an unknown destination. Then we see film of this happening, this enormous waddling blob barely able to squeeze out through his own front door, being escorted across the lawn by a couple

Garvey Quinn

of TNT security guards, all the time holding a towel over his face so you never get to see what he really looks like. A kind of sling's put on him and he's winched up into the helicopter like a baby elephant in a wildlife doco, and finally they show us the chopper flying away. Then it's back to the newsreader, who says, Bryan Mars is now at an unknown destination. It is not yet known who provided the helicopter that snatched him away from the media spotlight.

I turn the TV off and sit there stunned by what I've just seen of Bryan Mars. I mean there's fat and there's really fat and then there's disgusting, but even that doesn't do him justice. How could anybody let themselves go like that, no matter how much of a pile of shit they think life might be? At least the movie version doesn't call for me to get that fat, and I'll make damn sure they stick to their contract about getting me a personal trainer and top medical advice and I'll work like a bastard to get back in trim, fucking oath I will.

The idea consoles me, makes me feel a bit more settled. Probably all that hard work I'm doing in the pool now is standing me in good stead for later when I have to get the weight off again, sort of like money in the fitness bank. I get the urge to go and crank out thirty or forty laps, even though Arthur Snow hasn't told me anything about my schedule for this week. Once filming started we tapered off the training, just enough to keep condition up without leaving me too buggered to act as well, but with things on hold, there's nothing to say I can't just go down to the Aquatic Centre and do it for myself. As I go into the bedroom to get my Speedos and my trackie, I'm already feeling the sensation, arm through low and deep, one two three four breathe, kick, kick, kick, kick, arm through, and I'm even starting to savour that chlorine smell. Then the phone rings.

Stuie's on the other end. How you going Garvey?

Not bad, mate. Was just on my way out to the pool to get a few laps in.

Don't you fucking dare! You so much as put a toe in the water I'll kill you, if Stirling Seagrave doesn't do it first.

What?

Seagrave's people have just been in touch, he tells me, calming down a bit. They say they've got enough in the can to make the pool sequences work. You've got to stop swimming and start eating, big time.

It seems that Seagrave's doubts about my competence don't stop at my acting ability. Even my eating is to be managed, though I've seen enough guys turn themselves into lardarses to know that all it takes is a truckload of takeaways and VB. I'm taken to meet Dr Roland Gussett, introduced to me as THE Hollywood specialist in actors' weight gain and loss, flown over by the producers specially to look after me. I probably should feel honoured, but I'm a little worried by his appearance. He's definitely on the roly-poly side, wearing those funny high-waisted trousers that tubby blokes wear to try to make themselves look stocky rather than fat. I worry that his expertise only runs as far as getting the weight on, not taking it off. He sees me staring at him.

I have a glandular condition, he tells me. In my case calorie intake and output is unconnected with body mass.

Oh, I say, sorry, like I believe him.

I'm shown diets charts and calorie ratings and graphs of projected gain per day, but it looks like the sort of stuff that baffled me when I had to do science at school. All I want is for him to tell me what to eat. Eventually he does, and like I expected there's a lot of takeaways, and I'm given a gold pass to KFC. Why especially KFC? I ask. Gussett proves to be one more person who looks at me like I'm an idiot whenever I ask a question.

GARVEY QUINN

Because that's what Bryan Mars eats.

For variety there's also a lot of turkey and pork, pizza and deep fried fish and chips, and dessert is taken care of too, mostly chocolate cake, Tim Tams and ice-cream, in quantities that don't seem possible. To avoid unnecessary exercise, all of this is to be delivered, along with a standing order from the local bottle shop, of several slabs of VB per week. I like to eat and drink as much as the next bloke, within reason, but as I tell the doctor, all this looks beyond me. He opens his briefcase and takes out an array of little bottles filled with tablets and capsules, some of them large enough to choke a horse.

When these kick in, you'll practically be eating in your sleep.

This is all very well, but I'm concerned about the long-term effects. I ask him, do you have ones that will make me stop eating when this is all over?

Well yes and no.

What the fuck does that mean?

Pharmacology does exist to reverse the process, but at this stage it's not nearly as advanced. And when a patient's put on as much weight as you're going to have to, getting it off again is still largely a matter of willpower and hard work. But you *will* be supervised.

I don't like the sound of any of this, especially not hearing myself described as a patient. But before I can say anything more, the doctor is heading for the door, offering a quick handshake as he goes.

Don't worry, he tells me. I've worked with some of the greats.

Did you work with de Niro?

Not directly. But John Candy was a close personal friend, God rest his soul.

I'm thinking, I've got to place my life in this guy's hands? He reacts to the look on my face.

Though I should stress, John was not one of my clients per se. If he had been, perhaps he'd still be with us today, poor soul.

★ ★ ★

Even before I begin the diet, with the first food delivery not due until the following morning, I start to feel bloated and slow moving. All I can do is sit around the flat, occasionally flicking the TV on and off, hoping for something undemanding, but mostly just staring at nothing in particular. When Madeleine comes back from the pool I can see she's on one of those training highs you get sometimes, exhausted to the bone yet somehow tingling with the excitement of it all, apparently due to something called endorphins being secreted. It's an experience that's off-limits to me now, and I feel envious, and too dulled to give Madeleine much of a greeting. Perhaps it's the high she's on, but right away she senses what I'm feeling.

Run with it, Garvey. Let it take you completely.

What?

I can see it beginning for you. As it must have for Bryan Mars. At some point, while he was still the perfect, golden hero, there must have been a moment when he glimpsed the other side and thought, do I have the strength to hold on?

Poor bastard.

Only when you feel the truth about Bryan Mars, when you follow him into that same fearful nothingness, will you be able to do justice to the role.

Oh.

Garvey Quinn

And I'm privileged to be so close to you at a moment like this. My whole being is tingling with the awe of it.

I'm hoping this is Madeleine's over-complicated way of saying she's on for a root. Real swimmers are supposed to change out of their wet gear at the end of a session, have a hot shower and rug up well to guard against muscle stiffnesss, but on a warm day, Madeleine's just thrown a sarong round herself and driven home. I reach for the end of the sarong where she's tucked it in under itself and begin to peel it off her. Her swimmers, cut high at the thigh and made of material so thin you can almost see skin through it, cling to her with moisture. The months of swimming have broadened her shoulders and defined a whole lot of muscles that I wasn't aware of when I first saw her in the raw, and her stomach now has tight ripples that get me boned up just thinking about them. I put a hand up under the material where it swoops up at the top of her leg, reaching for hair, then for wetness, and with the other hand roll the suit down off her shoulders. I home in on her spot more or less right away and soon she's moaning like I've never heard her before, maybe it's those endorphins, and I jump up and rip my own clothes off so fast I wreck the zip of my jeans. But as I sink into her, I feel as if I'm watching it all from somewhere else, and wondering, how much nookie will I get when I look like the barrel off a Pioneer concrete truck? Will I even be able to find my dick?

About a minute after it's all over, Madeleine drops off to sleep, like blokes are always getting accused of doing, and she doesn't even stir when the phone rings. It's Seagrave, who lately has been getting his lackeys to pass messages on to me, as if he's too important to talk to a mere actor, even one who's starring in his new movie.

How you doing, Garvey?

All right thanks, I answer. He's not usually this interested in how I'm doing.

I hope you realise that you're involved in something very very special. You should consider yourself priviliged.

Yeah, that's what Madeleine said.

She's a smart girl. Ever been to Darwin?

No, I tell him. All I know about Darwin is that my brother Dean was going to piss off up there when he got Jodie up the duff, but Dad told him to stay here and face it like a man, so they got married instead.

You'll love it. Get your bag packed and be on your doorstep at 6.30 tomorrow morning. I'll give you a lift to the airport.

Before I could ask anything more he'd hung up. I didn't sleep a wink, just lay there all night worrying about what I might have got myself in for, over and over again seeing that shot of poor Bryan Mars being winched into the helicopter, so big you wonder how it could even still fly. I think, what if I just say, sorry, I'm not going, I never agreed to this, and then just wait for the shit to hit the fan. Stuie's reaction I could handle, he'd say, you're finished in the profession, and I'd say, great, I'd rather be a plumber anyway. But Madeleine, no, how could I ever tell her that I wasn't prepared to go along with the great director and really stretch myself in pursuit of a truthful performance? She'd never speak to me again.

Now and again I lift the sheet up to sneak one more look at Madeleine's naked shape, flat on her back, each breath rippling through her, her stomach and her boobs rising and falling, and I can't escape the feeling that this could be the last time I'm allowed such a good view. I feel like I'm on the edge of something, and I want to hold onto her, but when I touch her all I get is a murmur, not like in the old days when we'd go at it all night and drop off to sleep with me still inside her.

★ ★ ★

In the morning Seagrave picks me up in an enormous American Dodge pickup truck, bright metallic red and towering over everything else on the road except the semis. I notice that since I saw him last the ponytail's gone and he's had his head completely shaved, all shiny and polished. Waiting at lights he keeps revving the Dodge's V10 engine and commanding me to listen to it, as if I had any choice.

Nine litres of raw power, he tells me. There's a time for subtlety and there's a time for sheer grunt, and that's what we're into now.

I suspect he's not just talking about his truck. When he hands over the keys at valet parking, he bawls out the kid who takes the keys from him when the kid pulls the driver's door open too wide and gently taps a plastic pipe.

One scratch on that and you're history, don't think I won't nail your arse to the wall!

On the flight to Darwin I'm sitting between Seagrave and the screenwriter, Nelson Flack. He'd be fifty plus, and his blond hair's too long for a bloke that age, thin and whispy, hanging down from his bald spot so it touches his shoulders. It's left a little sprinkle of dandruff on his bottle green corduroy jacket, which is a stupid thing to be wearing to Darwin anyway. I don't know why they didn't put me to one side of them, or maybe in the cargo hold, for all the attention they pay me, and when I come up in the conversation I'm referred to like I'm not there.

Then we get the guy to pack on another, say, fifteen kilograms for the suicide scene, Flack says, making notes the whole time. How long's that going to take?

Seagrave answers. The doc says about three weeks.

Couldn't he do better than that? Jesus Christ, for a two-minute scene.

I'll tell the doc to kick the guy's arse. I agree, speed's critical. I mean, we're going to use up so much time getting him to look the way Bryan Mars does now, we need to cut back anywhere we can.

Er, excuse me, but I thought I was only going to – Nelson Flack talks straight over me.

I mean, as I see it, the real impact is just how big this turkey's let himself become, how gross and degenerate, so these framing scenes with him looking back over what he once was and chowing down on a tub of chicken nuggets are what makes it. Without that, it's just another sporting story, and –

Seagrave snaps his fingers and Flack shuts up. Turkey, he says, as if a light bulb's gone on in his head.

Just an expression, says Flack.

I heard about this somewhere, animal rights were trying to ban it. They get these turkeys, to make pâté out of their livers.

I think that's geese.

OK, geese, turkeys, whatever. Point is they hook them up to this machine which kind of continuously injects them with corn and other stuff, and they say you can actually see them getting fatter, right before your eyes.

I see your point. Better get the doc onto it. Jesus, if we can just cut a couple of months off this.

This time I do manage to butt in. Being treated like a jerk is bad enough, but now they're talking about me like I'm just some farmyard animal.

Excuse me. The movie I signed up to do ended when he

disappeared on the beach. And I agreed to put on enough weight to look like he did at that point, not five years later with him looking like, well, a dump truck. I don't think this is fair.

Almost like they'd rehearsed it, the two of them look at me and repeat my word together, with the same sneer. Fair? Seagrave takes over.

You think fairness has anything to do with making movies, pal? With making great movies?

Yes I do.

When I said you're privileged, I meant it. Do you realise why I asked you to come along with us?

Not exactly. To meet Bryan Mars, I suppose.

Not just to meet him. To know him.

All right, meet him, know him, whatever you want to call it.

No Garvey, I don't think you understand. This is not just about shaking hands and talking football. You are going to leave Darwin inhabited by his spirit. What we're hoping for is one of the most extraordinary character transferrals in the history of cinema.

Once someone starts talking about the greatest this or that in the history of cinema you know you're up shit creek. As if I didn't know that already.

Nelson Flack takes over again. Garvey, since we found that Bryan Mars was alive, I've begun writing some new scenes which, I honestly believe – and I'm speaking here as a seasoned professional not given to tossing superlatives around lightly – which I honestly believe are quite extraordinary. And I am sure that Stirling will direct them in a way that is quite extraordinary. We are both rising to a very special occasion. As we are sure you will, young and inexperienced though you may be.

Inexperienced? I did three years on *Medical Emergency*.

Garvey, a part like this might come along once in an actor's lifetime. And it takes total commitment. It takes sacrifice. You have to put yourself right out there.

Seagrave chimes in.

Do a little research. Read up on how Meryl Streep worked her way into the role of Lindy Chamberlain.

I hate it when people do this to me, trotting out the name of someone really famous, like I'd be a fuckwit for not trying to do what they did.

Lindy Chamberlain didn't weigh three tonnes.

I think I'm about to get a breather when this grannyish-looking woman comes over holding a lunch menu and a pen. And it's me she wants, not them, however big deals they might think they are in the movie world, me, Garvey Quinn, the airhead soapie hack.

Mr Quinn, this is such an honour, and I want to tell you I think it was nothing short of criminal when they took *Medical Emergency* off the air, I wondered if you'd mind signing –

Seagrave brandishes his thick yellow notepad, using it as a barrier between me and my fan.

Can't you see we're hard at work here?

I'm terribly sorry, I –

The old lady cringes off, and I'm furious.

You had no right to treat her like that. I respect my public.

Those people are no longer your public, Seagrave tells me. We are about to bring you to a new public. And when you're old, looking back on a long and successful career, maybe with an Oscar or two, you'll remember this moment and you'll thank us. You'll thank us from the bottom of your heart.

★ ★ ★

GARVEY QUINN

Being the big shot he is, I'd expected Stirling Seagrave to have us picked up at Darwin airport by a stretch limo, or at the very least a decent Merc, but we're led to a grey Falcon, the model that got superseded two years ago. We go round a couple of city blocks, then into an underground carpark, and from there we get into what seems like a private lift. Next thing you know we're in the corridor of what must be an apartment block. I didn't know they had this stuff in Darwin, I thought it was all tin roofs and fibro.

Seagrave rings a buzzer and a woman answers the door. She's all dressed up, like she's probably gone to a lot of trouble because of us, maybe a new dress, bright pink, and a lot of make-up. Even though she's smiling hard, her mouth still turns down at the ends, like she's spent a lot of time worrying. Seagrave speaks first.

Mrs Mars. I want you to know just how much your co-operation means to us.

And what you people are doing means a lot to me. I always knew that one day someone would come along and recognise Bryan's greatness, I've always told Bryan that. Just keep believing in who you are and eventually it'll happen. And here you are.

Listening to her, seeing the eagerness on her face, I can't help thinking, Jesus, what that poor old duck must have gone through, no wonder she seems like a bit of a fruitcake. But I'm pleased to find she's not so batty she doesn't recognise a star when she meets one.

Garvey Quinn. What a pleasure.

The pleasure's mine.

And I want to tell you, there's no one in the world I'd rather see playing my son. You're so perfect for the part, it's almost like the two of you must be long lost brothers.

That's when I see my long lost soul brother, Bryan Mars,

not bothering to get up off the sofa to greet his visitors. And why would he, with all that weight to shift? I move towards him, a funny feeling coming over me, creepy, because it's like I'm looking at the me that's ahead of me, if you see what I mean. It's not until you get up close to him, in the flesh, that you can really take in what he's like. The shot of him on the news just didn't do him justice. He's sort of like a big soft ball, like a beanbag, spreading over the sofa, which is soft itself, so it's closing up around him and you can't exactly be sure which is the furniture and which is him. All around the apartment, which they can't have been in for more than a day, his mother has taped up these photographs of Bryan in his heyday, that sleek body, even sleeker than mine, poised on the starting block, balanced on just his toes, or leaping high out of the water, punching the air after a world record. Like I say, it gives me the creeps, but I try to act normal, the way you're supposed to when you're with people who've got something wrong with them, not let on that you've noticed anything. That's a lesson I learned early in life, when my dad whacked me over the ear for pointing out a bloke at the footy with an artificial nose.

How you going? I'm Garvey Quinn.

He accepts my handshake, and I think I hear a g'day, but it's pretty obvious he doesn't want any of this. He probably doesn't have much choice, though, as it looks like some sort of deal's been done, the producers putting him up in this maximum security apartment in return for him co-operating on the story. Not that I can be sure, because as usual nobody's bothered to tell me anything, I'm just an actor. My only instructions are to watch him closely, try to pick up any little mannerisms that'll help me construct the character, but how many mannerisms can you pick up from watching a doona? Seagrave gets straight down to business, like he's conducting a meeting in his office, not dropping in on somebody's home.

Bryan, I want you to know, you're in safe hands. We have the utmost respect for you as a human being. Your story will be treated sensitively, and with dignity. We're not into fat jokes, we're serious film makers, trying to tell an important story for our times.

Mars doesn't respond, but right away his mum pipes in.

Bryan understands. He had a lot to do with people in the entertainment world when he was in the limelight you know, was a bit of a TV star himself, so he knows how you creative people work.

I remember from the scrapbooks they gave me to look through that at one stage Mars was being screen-tested to do guest interviews on *Sports World*, and then after the shark business there was even talk of an aquatic adventure show, *Bryan Mars's World of the Deep*. Or *Bryan Mars Plumbs the Depths*, as somebody called it, after everything had gone wrong.

Flack assists with the sales pitch. And while, yes, we inevitably have to portray some of the bad things that happened, we won't be dwelling on them. In the end, I see this as a story about the indestructibility of the human spirit.

There's not a flicker of reaction from Bryan, but Mrs Mars is beaming. That was my one worry, you know, when I first heard that someone was going to make a movie of Bryan's life. That they'd forget about his wonderful achievements in the pool and just concentrate on the difficulties he had once he got a little bit of a weight problem. The way some of those comedians on TV made fun of him. It was shameful, falling into swimming pools in their silly padded suits and everything, and we would have hated to see you bring in some overweight actor and dig up that stuff all over again.

Bryan's problems are in the past, and that's where they should stay.

Yes.

But when I heard Garvey Quinn was going to play Bryan, then I knew we'd be all right.

I'll do my very best, I can assure you.

Mrs Mars goes over to one of the cardboard boxes that cover a tabletop, with nothing much unpacked after what must have been a rushed move. I see her riffle through a stack of magazines and pull out a copy of *New Idea*. I know right away which one it must be, which page she's going to open up. She holds up that great picture of me, grinning as I step out of the pool, dripping water and every muscle rippling, it gave me a shock when I saw it, just how much the training had done for me, and my Speedos nearly falling off.

This is how Bryan should be shown to the world, she tells us all, even tells Bryan, who doesn't look like he has any thoughts on the subject at all. It's sinking in that neither of them knows what Seagrave really has in mind, about my bloating right out to play Bryan in hiding, looking back over his life. I've been told not to say anything about what we're doing, but I thought that was just to keep me in my place. Then the door buzzer rings, and Mrs Mars gets up to answer it. She's back half a minute later with one of those super family size plastic KFC buckets, the sort I'm going to have to get used to.

Mid-afternoon snack delivery, she tells us as she plonks it down in front of Bryan. Sometimes Bryan gets a bit peckish before dinner.

Seagrave asks her, all the arrangements working out OK?

Yes, thank you so much for helping us out. I'll tell you, those last two days, after Bryan got discovered, they were hell on earth, it was like living in a goldfish bowl.

Only too glad to assist. It's in everybody's interests that you and Bryan should feel as comfortable as possible. If there's anything else you need, you just have to ask.

Thank you. Thank you so much. Honestly, I feel so much confidence in you people, you're like a gift from heaven. I mean, I don't know much about movie making, but I do know that you wouldn't have chosen Garvey Quinn to play my son if you weren't very special people.

We never even considered anybody else, Seagrave tells her.

Of course, something was bound to happen sooner or later, you know, she goes on. I always knew, one day Bryan wouldn't be able to contain himself any longer, he'd step out that door, and when that happened somebody would be bound to recognise him, he was that well known.

So that was the first time he'd been outside the place in, how long? asks Seagrave.

Since we moved there. Three years. We had to leave the previous place when a swimming coach moved in next door, if we'd stayed there, Bryan would have been a goner.

I see Nelson Flack making notes. He pulls his chair a bit closer to Bryan before he talks, so that Mrs Mars isn't between them. I'm watching Bryan as he gets going on the KFC, watching for mannerisms. I see that he likes to put two chicken nuggets into his mouth at a time, and he puts two more in before he's finished swallowing the first lot. I wonder if I should write this down, or just hope I remember later. Nelson Flack speaks in a low, serious voice like one of the older doctors on *Medical Emergency*.

Bryan, what's important is that I get to hear your story in your words. I'm the writer, but it's your voice that must come through. Do you think you can help me?

Bryan's answer comes through the thick wad of chicken

pulp that's mulling around in his mouth. Um-uh.

Great. Great. You see Bryan, like everyone else we assumed you'd drowned that day you left your clothes on the beach. But once we heard you were still alive, we realised we could give our film a whole new dimension that would lift it way above every other sports movie that's been made. We'll get to see all your great feats, and your trials and tribulations, the price of fame, all of that, but we'll see it through your eyes. As we see you ploughing up the pool on the way to a world record, or accepting your medal for bravery, we'll hear the voice of the mature Bryan Mars, looking back over it, trying to put it all into perspective. It's that voice-over that's going to make the film something special, but you and you alone can make it happen. I'm just a servant. A servant of the truth.

This is bullshit. I've seen enough of the new script to know that this is an absolute lie. Sure there's going to be a voice-over, but it's going to be over the Darwin scenes with me at maximum weight, like the one where I'm wobbling through a shopping centre carpark with a slab of beer on each shoulder, pursued by a horde of thong-clapping rednecks. I turn and throw the beer cartons back at them, and flatten a little kid with one, a cute little kid with an autograph book, like I used to be so nice to in the old days. Then there's a scene where Mum brings in a wheelbarrow full of Kentucky Fried and I keep on eating until even I, Bryan Mars the bottomless pit, can't hold anymore, but I force one more nugget in with the back of a spoon and it pops back out again. I think they've stolen it from some movie where a guy explodes.

So, says Flack, I've got to find out what it was like here, what you were thinking all that time. I mean, there must have been so much going on in your head, with a past like yours, so many highs and lows to flash back to. It'd be almost like a non-stop movie, would I be right?

Um, no.

Mrs Mars can't keep herself out of it any longer.

Bryan's always been very modest about things. Never made a big fuss about what he achieved, and never moaned when things went wrong.

Flack keeps prodding.

That's all very well, but it doesn't make for much of a story. I mean, for someone to need to disappear from the world so much that they'd fake a suicide. There's got to be a lot of mental turmoil there.

Um, I suppose. Um-uh. He might have been saying a word or two more, for all anyone knows, but he'd shoved three chicken nuggets into his gob simultaneously.

Seagrave joins in again. Bryan, I wonder if that might be the key to unlocking all this. If you can share that moment with us, that cold, windy day when you swam out to sea. Did you really mean to die, and then find you couldn't go through with it?

Um, sort of. Don't know.

Seagrave and Flack are starting to give little private groans at each other now, with each disappointing answer from Bryan. I wish they could just leave the guy alone, I mean how would you feel if someone asked you about trying to kill yourself? But Flack just pushes on.

Because at that moment, on that beach, you created the life you've lived ever since. And we need to know what that felt like, to deny your own identity, and yet have to live every day in the shadow of it. I'm asking you to dig deep into your soul, Bryan.

What Bryan's digging deep into is the KFC bucket. Flack doesn't probe any more, but starts writing. Just getting a few thoughts together, he explains as he scribbles. I'm sure we can find a way into this somehow.

Mrs Mars gets up and goes to another one of the cardboard boxes and after a moment's poking around comes back with a scrapbook.

I've never shown you this before, Bryan, it's the things I collected after you went missing, from all the newspapers and magazines, the tributes to you, and the long articles warning about the pressures they put on young sports people these days. I never showed it to you because I know you don't like looking back at the bad things. But I thought maybe now it'd jog your memory a bit, I mean we do want to help these nice people, don't we Bryan, love. They're only trying to do their job. Look, here, there's all the people standing looking out to sea, look, there's Arthur Snow, and there's Alexander Morton, such an important man, but he was so kind, he went out of his way to personally pick me up in his Rolls-Royce. And look, there's the minister for sport, and there's at least three Olympic champions, all of them with tears streaming down their faces. And look, there's me.

Did you know, Mrs Mars? That Bryan wasn't dead? Seagrave asks the same question I've been wondering about.

Not then, no. I was in a dreadful state. I was as much in the dark as anybody. Then a few days later I got a letter, it said find us a house in Darwin, see you in three months, with just a post office box number. After that I was able to just watch them all, happy that Bryan had got the last laugh. Then she jabs her finger into a spot on the page, and her voice becomes harsher.

Ooh, look there. It's her. She didn't think any of us knew she was there, but I did. See, with the scarf round her head and her collar pulled up and everything. Ooh, by gee, I'm sorry to have to say this, Bryan, but that girl has a lot to answer for, that Vicki Michaels.

GarVEY QUiNN

You hear about people in emergencies lifting a whole car off someone single-handed, and that's sort of what Bryan Mars does at that moment, lifting his entire carcass off the sofa in one go, when it looks like it'd be a job for a mobile crane. For the first time a real voice comes out of him, and it's a horrifying No-ooooooo as he grabs the scrapbook out of his mum's hands and throws it on the floor and stamps on it.

We all just stare silently for a minute or two, until Mrs Mars says, perhaps Bryan's had enough excitement for one day. Perhaps we all have.

We're scheduled to stay another couple of days, have some more meetings, but Seagrave rebooks us on the next flight out of Darwin. And though I thought he and Nelson Flack would be spitting chips about the way things turned out, what with Bryan being so hopeless, they look surprisingly happy. One of them has bought a magazine at the airport, and there's yet another big spread about Bryan Mars, not just the movie now, but the fact that he isn't dead, with the headline, Tragic champion – the man who wouldn't die. There's a picture of me, and one of Madeleine, more pool shots in our swimmers, but most of it's the real thing, Bryan winning, modest Bryan after the rescue, Bryan with blood streaming down his face after the nightclub punch-up. And slightly chubby Bryan shedding tears and trying to avoid the camera after he's missed the Olympic team. This isn't what interests Seagrave and Flack though. The whole of one page is taken up by a shot of Bryan's girlfriend, Vicki Michaels, and it's a shot I remember, one from an Olympic calendar with them all in the raw. The way she's posed, you can't quite see nipples or pubes, not quite, but Christ is she built. Everything's perfect, the curve under her boobs, the way the top of her thigh muscle comes up to meet her stomach, which is not quite rounded yet not quite flat, the ripples coming up under the rib cage. It makes me think of Madeleine, the day before I flew out, all around me and all over me, her skin sticking to mine, so giving and so excited, and all for me. Remembering her like that, I'm sure that after, when she wouldn't respond when I ran my hand up her thigh, she was just tired from all the swimming, it was nothing to do with feelings.

Look at her, just look at her, Seagrave is saying. No wonder he lost his marbles when she gave him the flick. Christ, if I perv on her much longer I'm going to have to slip down the aisle for a J Arthur Rank.

Yeah, me too, I hear Flack agree, and I can see both of them have their laps covered the same way I do, only they haven't bothered to take their hands away from middle stump. Flack goes on.

Once he packed a few kilos on, and she stayed like that, that must have been the end of him. I mean a girl who looked like that wouldn't let herself be rooted by anything less than perfection. Poor guy, she was probably revolted by him. And the story was that when he was in top shape, the two of them used to just go at it hammer and tongs, anywhere they could, in any spare locker room they could find, in showers, in his Beemer out in the carpark. They were just completely animal, nearly got chucked off the team for it.

Why the fuck isn't that in the script?, Seagrave demands. All we've got are a few kisses and cuddles.

Because the money guys were worried about the rating.

Fuck the rating, let's go for it.

Let's go for it.

At that point I see them both turn to me, as if they're sizing me up to see if I'm man enough for some job they've got planned. Seagrave asks, Garvey, mate, how are things between you and the lovely Madeleine?

I'm not sure what he means. Not sure I want to know.

Er, just fine.

Nelson, how good are you at writing sex scenes?

I can write them with one hand. In fact, I normally do.

I think I've got it, says Seagrave. How I see it is this. What's really going round and round in Bryan's mind as he slobs around in the Darwin house and eats his way through half the food output of a small Third World country is all the shagging he's missed out on with Vicki. And all the shagging he had with her, replay after replay. That's what he's obsessed with, not the records or anything, but bonking Vicki. So the voice-over, even over scenes of him stumbling through Darwin with his crate of VB, will be stuff along the lines of, you know, she was hot and wet as I spread her out on the stack of towels and whipped out my plonker for the tenth time that day. That style of thing, anyway, Nelson, I'm sure you can write something better than that.

I'm sure I can too.

And we've got to hold off this guy's fat diet just a little longer, I'm afraid, because we've got to re-shoot a lot of the pool scenes so it's sex, sex, sex. Garvey, you and Madeleine are going to do some of the most real looking sex scenes ever, they'll be so real people will swear you were actually doing it. How do you feel about that?

Er, just fine.

★ ★ ★

When the script's finalised, a courier brings copies round to the flat, one for me and one for Madeleine. She sits down on the sofa to read hers, and I want to join her, somehow it seems like a good idea to read it together. But as soon as I snuggle up to her and put my arm round her, my head close to hers so I can look at her script, she stands up and shoves her script back in its folder.

Sorry Garvey, I have to get into the part, it's a private thing.

So Madeleine takes her script into the bedroom and shuts the door behind her, while I stay on the sofa with my copy. It doesn't take me long to work out there's a hell of a lot of rooting in the new script, lots of descriptions of swimsuits being peeled off wet panting bodies, hands going up thighs, legs wrapped round waists, bare bums pumping, nipples in mouths, plenty of groaning and shrieking and heads thrown back in ecstasy, and lines like, give it to me, now, harder, harder, Oh God yes! It's not difficult to work out what Nelson Flack was doing with his other hand – in fact, what it reminds me of most is the video one of my brother Dean's plumber mates brought along to his bucks' night.

When I've finished I push the bedroom door open a few inches, not wanting to interrupt Madeleine too suddenly, knowing how involved she gets in her work.

So, what do you think, I ask her?

Madeleine gives me a really hard look, as if she's annoyed at something, though I can't tell whether it's me or the script or something else in her life I just don't know about.

We'll just have to do our best, Garvey. We just have to hope that somewhere in that squalid meat market we can find a way to give the audience a glimpse of something higher, if we give enough of ourselves as actors.

* * *

Seagrave has assured me he's going to shoot the new sex scenes on a closed set, but this turns out to mean that only about half the usual number of hangers-on are around the place, and I still feel pretty exposed when I drop my Speedos. I keep a towel around me between takes, trying to keep it on until the very last moment before the cameras roll, but the problem is that no matter how hard I try to stop myself getting barred up, it keeps happening, and I know it's showing through. They're not actually going to show my donger on film, at least I don't think they are, but all the same it worries me, and I know Dad would kill me, he'd call me a flasher and a pervert, put it away, son, do you think anyone wants to look at that sort of thing? Actually they do, judging by some of the looks I'm getting.

The situation isn't helped by the way Madeleine is carrying on. She's done plenty of nudity on stage and she's very comfortable having people look at her body, so comfortable that between takes she's in no hurry to put on the dressing gown they've given her, if she even bothers at all. So I've got all that in front of me all the time, reminding me of what I was doing to her just a minute before. We're doing a scene where Bryan and Vicki have found a change room no one's using, and gone in and locked it behind them. They're both really pumped up from a heavy training session, they've got to have it, right now, and as soon as the door shuts behind them they're into it, gear ripped off and a few towels thrown on the concrete floor for Vicki's comfort, him on top, me that is, her legs wrapped right round. One camera's hanging from the roof, looking straight down on top, and another two are at ground level, one in front, one at the back. It's the one at the back that worries me, because a couple of times I can't help myself, I actually get it into Madeleine, mumbling sorry, sorry, as I pull it out at the end of the take, and grabbing for that towel as fast as I can. Madeleine doesn't seem to mind, or if she does she's too professional to show it. At the end of each take I hear her asking Seagrave, how was that?

What happens next in the new version of the script is that Arthur Snow has got wind of what's going on and he's terrified Bryan's performance in the pool is going to suffer. Arthur finds a key to the change room, and he lets himself in just as we're both coming, Vicki screaming her lungs out and me shouting yes, yes, yes. In one version Nelson Flack had me shouting gold, gold, gold, but for some reason Seagrave made him change it. Anyway, in the script, Arthur Snow is ropeable, and he puts most of the blame on Vicki Michaels. There and then, he chucks her out of his elite training squad, though everybody says that in real life Snow actually threw her out because he wanted some action himself but she wouldn't come across. He's technical adviser on the movie, so I suppose they had to watch themselves.

Duncan Young, who's playing Arthur Snow, seems to be really enjoying himself. He's extending that moment after he's pushed the door open and we're still so heavily into it we don't know he's there and just keep going at it hammer and tongs while he looks down at us. And I hear the door open, and I know he's standing there, three feet away, perving for all he's worth, but I'm not allowed to react until I hear him shout, you two are a disgrace to the world of swimming! The world that's given you everything! As we do retake after retake, the time between the door opening and him saying his lines gets longer and longer. Which makes it even more embarrassing whenever I lose control of myself.

Even worse, Duncan Young, who makes no secret of the fact that he's noticed what's going on, likes to come and sit next to me between takes, swigging on his flask while I try to carefully arrange my hands over the bump under my towel. He gives me professional advice, the old hand passing on a few tips to the new boy.

Jack Nicholson told me that when he was doing the shagging scenes with Jessica Lange in *The Postman Always Rings Twice*, sometimes between takes to ease the situation he'd duck outside and bop the baloney. Have a colourful turn of phrase, don't they, those Americans, he says.

Yes they do.

Duncan goes on and on, sitting right up close breathing out whisky fumes and nudging me in the ribs.

Anyway, that might be a little trick you could consider. Another chap I knew used to put a tight rubber band round his member, used to find that helped keep it from rearing its ugly head when things got a bit exciting on the set. Only problem was, one day he forgot to take it off afterward. Went out for a night on the hops and woke up the next morning, you know the way a fellow does, full of piss with a big aching boner. Well, let me tell you dear boy, the doctors said he was just minutes away from gangrene setting in.

That's very interesting, I say.

At last Seagrave decides the scene will do. There are a couple more new scenes, these ones thankfully without Duncan Young involved. In one we do it standing up in a shower, and in the other we're in the front seat of my BMW in the carpark, and nearly get sprung by a photographer. We only escape by pulling our heads down and driving away starkers, Madeleine still spread out over my lap, her bum still bouncing up and down just below the dashboard. As soon as I've driven the car safely out of shot Madeleine wriggles off my lap like someone who's just discovered they're sitting on an ants' nest.

This isn't exactly the film we signed up for, she murmurs, not looking my way.

It's not what I had in mind either.

StUffED

Each night, Madeleine and I both just get into bed and fall into a deep sleep, hardly bothering to touch each other, often not even saying goodnight. In her case it could be partly because she's stepped up her training schedule, far more than she needs to for the role, which I suppose shows just how professional she's become. In my case, I just feel strange. Tomorrow I have to start eating.

Seagrave, with expert advice from Roland Gussett, was worried that if I started my eating binge even a couple of days too early, some slight hint of weight gain might be noticeable in the sex scenes. As Seagrave put it, nobody's going to pay to watch flab rooting. But with the sex out of the way, I have no choice but to get down to some serious eating. People start arriving with food, first at breakfast where a cook comes in and fries piles of eggs and bacon, plus a lot of American-style stuff, those big heavy, buttery pancakes and hash browns. I'm not used to eating that kind of thing, and looking at it puts me off at first. When I tell the cook, one of Roland Gussett's team flown in specially to look after me, he smiles the way dentists do when they're getting the drill ready.

Trust me. We Americans are better at putting on weight than anyone else in the world. Even Sumo wrestlers come to us for help now.

Despite my early doubts, I find that once I start eating, I really get into it. I just love the feeling of more and more food going down, in a way that I've never known before. I just don't want it to stop, and I feel a little disappointed when there's no more on the table and the cook is washing up the dishes. Madeleine, enjoying her usual small bowl of muesli and freshly cut fruit with yoghurt on top, has been silent all through breakfast, occasionally glancing up as I flip another whole fried egg off the fork and into my mouth, or roll up a syrupy pancake with half a tub of butter inside it, but mostly averting her eyes. Now, as I wash it all down with a big mug of coffee with double cream and six sugars and give a loud burp, she stares at me in a way I haven't seen before, almost like she doesn't quite recognise me. Then she gives me a little smile, the sort of smile that looks like she had to do it deliberately.

Sorry, she tells me, it's just a bit of a shock to the system. But we're both going to have to keep art at the forefront of our minds.

Yes, I say, yes we are. As if I believe her, as if I believe that anything can save us now, other than a lightning bolt.

★ ★ ★

The same week I start pigging out, they're filming the rescue scenes on the beach, plus my fight with the artificial shark in a big tank at the studio. Nobody's too worried about my showing a bit of weight in that short time, but luckily I don't have to do much swimming as I already feel a bit heavy, already just feel like lying around doing nothing. So far the scales haven't shown any weight gain, though they say this is normal for someone starting off as fit as I am and in a week or two it'll hit me like a ton of bricks.

For the rescue scenes in the surf, they're using a double for me, an iron man champion, so all I have to do is stagger from the surf a few times, dragging out people I've rescued and then heading back in for more. The iron man does all the swimming out through the surf, to the reef where Alexander Morton's enormous cruiser is breaking up. We filmed the party scenes ages ago on a mock-up of the boat back at the studio, where Bryan gets to meet all these biggies, business tycoons like Morton and their facelifted wives, and actors more famous than me, plus a lot of those girls in bikinis who don't seem to do anything much but turn up where there's a top party. In this company, everybody thinks they're a star, so for a change, Bryan's just one of the crowd. That is until a storm comes up suddenly and the boat turns over on a reef, and suddenly he's the only one they look to. Stripping to his underdaks, Bryan saves the day.

For the wreck scenes they've disguised an impounded Taiwanese fishing trawler and stuck it out on Long Reef. The iron man has to swim back and forth through the surf, plucking another desperate partygoer off the side of the boat and dragging them back to the shore. Sometimes when some tubby businessman gets hysterical, Bryan has to punch him out, or in the case of a woman, slap her across the face to bring her to her senses. At some point, just beyond where the waves break, I take back the role, and get to drag in a succession of extras in dinner suits or evening dresses. In the case of the women, the good-looking ones anyway, Seagrave makes sure that just as they come out of the surf, either in my arms or staggering to their feet, the evening dress has slipped down to show at least one boob.

Then, with just one person to be rescued, Alexander Morton himself, one of the country's richest men, I'm about to charge back into the surf when the huddled group of survivors gasp. Shark! Out in the water the technical guys have started up the little radio-controlled submarine with the over-sized white pointer fin sticking up out of the waves, and it's zig-zagging through the surf, exactly where I have to swim to get back out to the boat. But I don't hesitate for a moment, diving back into the surf with a look of steel on my face.

Once I've disappeared under the waves, I can come back out again, and wait for my last surf scene for the day, where

Garvey Quinn

I bring gasping, near-death Alexander Morton in to the shore. Before that happens, the iron man has to outswim the shark on the way out to the boat but on the way back, weighed down by the tycoon, has no choice but to stand and fight. Ditching Morton for a moment he goes under, at the same moment as the technical guys put the fin into a dive. There's a flurry of splashing, and the survivors on the shore hold their breath for what seems like an eternity, until I, or Bryan, or actually the iron man in this case, bob up triumphant and resume hauling Morton back to shore.

By the time I've taken over hauling Morton out of the water I'm feeling so sluggish I can hardly move, and also incredibly hungry. Because filming took longer than expected, lunch is late, and my stomach is growling as I drag myself towards the catering truck, not the usual big one that everybody eats from, but my own personal one, with my own private dining room inside, and the imported cook hard at work at the deep fryer. I start off with a Texan specialty, chicken fried steak, which Roland Gussett swears by, thick steak cooked in chicken fat, mountains of fried potatoes, plenty of eggs on the side, then buckets of chocolate and crunchy butterscotch ice-cream, my favourite. It's so satisfying, all this eating, more satisfying than I ever believed possible, and for one tiny moment I think, I shouldn't be liking this so much, this is supposed to be just a job, be careful, but that thought dies with another mouthful of ice-cream.

When it's over I lie down on the sofa, and begin to doze off. Seagrave himself comes to check on me, and seems amused at the sight of me slowly waking up and dragging myself upright.

Really getting into the part, hey Garvey?

In the afternoon there's a just a bit of tidying up, a shot of me exhausted on the beach, standing in the background while Alexander Morton does this rave to a news crew about what an incredible hero I am and how big the shark was. Then I'm seen shrugging off help from an ambulance man, shaking Morton's hand but declining a lift in his private chopper, saying, after all this I've got to clear my head, and heading off for a lonely walk down the windswept beach. They make me keep walking and walking until I must only be a pinprick on the screen, and it's all I can do to keep up the pace they want. I know for sure my swimming days are over, and I wonder if Bryan Mars might have had the same thought, even then. All I'm thinking of is tonight's dinner. I wonder when he first started thinking about food all the time.

The next day we're to do just one more scene, the battle with the shark in the tank, and after that I'll have several weeks of doing nothing but sit around eating and watching my gut get bigger. When all this first started, that prospect would have disgusted me, but somehow, now, I find it really exciting, and when I wake up breakfast is the first thing on my mind, a big breakfast, even bigger than yesterday.

Roland Gussett doesn't disappoint. This morning he's sent the cook along with orders to prepare bigger pancakes, more eggs, thicker, fattier bacon, plus some interesting German sausages I haven't tried before, and it all goes down really well. What I like, too, is the smell of it, those heavy, pungent cooking smells that seem to hang in the air, the bacon and the sausages especially.

Madeleine, though, doesn't seem so impressed. First of all she joins me at the table with her bowl of muesli, but as soon as the smells come wafting in from the kitchen she gets up and throws open all the windows. She sits down again and has a go at eating, but the look on her face as the first spoonful of muesli goes into her mouth makes me wonder if she's going to be sick. By this time I'm chomping on a thick rasher of bacon, and as I do a lot these days, I keep on eating while I speak to her.

Everything OK? I ask.

She glares at me and bangs her spoon down on the table.

Don't you know it's rude to talk with your mouth full? I feel like I'm at a pig trough.

This seems a bit much, especially under these circumstances. Right now my job is to eat, and if I didn't talk with food in my mouth, I'd hardly get to talk at all.

Sorry, I tell her, though I'm still eating when I say it.

To be honest, I didn't think you had it in you to go this far for your art, she adds.

I didn't either, I tell her, still with a mouth full of food.

She gets up from the table and takes her bowl with her.

It's such a lovely day I think I'll get some fresh air, she says.

Madeleine takes her muesli out onto the balcony, but I don't feel like getting up to join her. Once I sit down to eat, I don't feel like moving again, so I just look at her through the window, admiring how beautiful she looks in her nightie, the really clingy one she likes to wear around the flat even when the cook is there.

★ ★ ★

From the first moment I sighted the fake shark I've had an uneasy feeling about it, and not just because of its size, though that's giving me food for thought as well. The thing is nearly as big as the shark in *Jaws*, and if the one that Bryan Mars tackled was really that size, I don't know how he could have done it, but that side of things is really none of my business, and I've already got enough stuff to worry about.

They'd already shown me how the shark worked, and got me to stand in waist-deep water while all its little motors whirred and it thrashed around one way and then the other, its jaws opening and closing, and I swung a few punches at it. For the filming, though, it has to be completely underwater, and I have to be as well, in a huge glass tank. They're not using a double because they want a lot of close-up shots of the determination on my face and the last bubbles of air escaping from my mouth. So I'm having to get used to keeping my eyes open underwater and it's quite a job, that plus acting at the same time, if you can call fighting with a plastic shark acting.

The fight has been carefully choreographed, and I've rehearsed the moves several times outside the tank, with a fight co-ordinator standing in for the shark. There's a lot of lunging, and dodging its jaw, but the crucial moment is when I gouge out one of its eyes and stun it with a king hit to the side of its head. I get some good holds on the fight co-ordinator, who's wearing a helmet, and I think I even see him stumble when I let go the king hit. I'm worried that it's going to be a lot more difficult doing it in the tank while holding my breath, but at least I know they have to let me win in the end.

Inside the tank, it's as different as I feared. It's fresh water, so it's harder to stay floating up near the top, where the shark is tethered. I keep sinking to the bottom, as if I'm wearing a weight belt, and it's a real effort to pull myself back up, as I wait for the shark to be set in motion. Several times it just doesn't work, and I'm signalled to come out while the problem is fixed. This just makes it harder, holding my breath for so long, over and over again, that plus the feeling of heaviness that I have all the time now, and which I really enjoy except when I have to do something.

GARVEY QUINN

Finally they get the shark working. I've got a tiny radio stuck in one ear, so I can hear Seagrave's instructions all too clearly. As the shark makes its moves I duck and dodge trying to get a clear strike at its eye, while Seagrave's shouting faster, what's wrong with you, come on, move your arse. When I come up for air between takes, he keeps on tearing strips off me, that was hopeless, if that shark was real he'd have had you for breakfast, you couldn't punch out a sardine.

This is really pissing me off, and I gasp back, if that shark was real he'd have anybody for breakfast, Bryan Mars included. Seagrave, though, isn't interested in any doubts I have about the authenticity of his film, and gets into a huddle with the technical guys. They come up with the idea of slowing down its motors, servos is apparently what they're called, that run all the little pistons that make it move in the sequence it's supposed to. So now I can go slow, to match the shark, and they'll speed up the film later. They make it pretty obvious this is not the way they'd like to be doing it.

There, says Seagrave. See how you go against a shark on Valium.

Even this needs several more takes than it should, partly because the shark's eyeball won't pop out cleanly the way it's supposed to when I stick my thumb in the socket, instead coming out in fragments of silicone, and they have to put in a new, higher density one. The tech guys are furious, though I can't for the life of me see how it could be my fault. One of them asks, do you know how long it took us to make that thing?

At last it all comes together, though even with the shark slowed down to jellyfish speed, I'm struggling to time my moves right. This time when I gouge my thumb in, the silicone eyeball pops out cleanly, but as I deliver the king hit, shouting at the thing, fuck you, Seagrave, I'm out of air, out of everything. I start to thrash, struggle, panicky, luckily not until a couple of seconds after the end of the shot, otherwise I'm sure they would have made me do it again, though I'm not sure I could. I can't get up high enough to reach the rim of the tank, and when I try to grab hold of the shark to lever myself out it's so slippery I slide right down its back, snagging my underdaks on its dorsal fin. As I struggle not to breathe in the mouthful of water I've got, I hear Seagrave through the earpiece, you can get out now, wonder boy.

The next thing I know I'm waking up, lying in a puddle on the tiles next to the tank, somebody's mouth is blowing into mine, and a circle of people are looking down on me, Seagrave among them. The medic props me up, and I vomit out a couple of lungfuls of water. Seagrave, half smiling, kneels down and pats me on the head.

Well, that's the easy part out of the way, he says. Now for the real hard work.

★ ★ ★

BRYAN MARS

You know they think you were shouting about Vicki, after your mum started talking about her like that. You know they think you've never got over it, poor bastard. They think you probably wank yourself stupid every night remembering what she was like, and you wonder what's going into the movie. They wanted you to say things about what's in your head, if you could have done that perhaps you could have controlled them a bit, controlled the movie, though the way that Stirling Seagrave looks, maybe not. What an arsehole he is. But you couldn't, because what's in your head isn't like that. There's no movie running continuously inside your brain, with the pool, Vicki, world records, the shark, the failure, the disgrace, playing over and over again, no matter where you are and what you're doing. It's like a blind's been pulled down in front of it all, and on that blind is written, this is what there is. And that's what you're looking at, however much you might be aware of what's behind it, however many of those magazines Mum might bring into the place.

So you just pace around, you don't lie around so much now, you feel like you want to keep your legs moving, as hard as that is. Round and round the apartment's big L-shaped living room, but especially out on the long balcony, up and down while you look over the edge at the street six floors down, where all those ordinary people are going about their business. You wonder, what do they feel like, what's it like to be down there, and you find yourself thinking, what if you just walked out, into the open, just stood there and let them all gawk at you as much as they wanted to, let them make all their jokes and poke at your rolls of fat until eventually they just get tired of it and all you are is one more gutso around the place.

But you can't, because they've got that covered, they've had it covered ever since that day they brought you here in the chopper and then the furniture van for the last stretch from the helipad. All you'd heard about the movie at that stage was what your mum had found in the *TV Week*, that nonentity of an actor, the sort you forget about a minute after you've seen the show. Then these guys in suits who turned up just after the van had delivered you told you a lot more than you wanted to hear. There was an angry one and a nice one, like they have in TV cop shows, and you could tell that the angry one didn't like being up in Darwin, he couldn't handle the heat or the people he was having to deal with, and he just wanted to get it over with and head down south. He was some kind of lawyer, but you could tell he was also something to do with movies, because he kept talking about the bottom line.

Mate, the bottom line is, this movie's going to be made, with or without your co-operation. Understand?

You wished you'd had your own lawyer there, like one of those sports management people who used to look after you, but all you had was your mum.

Um, yeah, you say, through your beard, not even able to look at them because you know they're looking at you.

And, let's face it pal, we wouldn't be shelling out big bucks putting you up in this place and keeping the media pack and the curiosity seekers at bay if we didn't expect something in return. Does that make sense to you?

Yeah, sort of.

Then his mate takes over, Mr Nice Guy.

Bryan, we know you've been through a lot, and we really feel for you. Right now you're very vulnerable, and our concern is that some people might try to take advantage of you, bring you back into the public eye before you're ready.

And before we're ready, more to the point, the angry one tells you.

Yeah, Right, Greg, thanks. And the thing is, Bryan, the movie will be made much better without that sort of complication. I'm sure you want the story of your life to be told properly, don't you?

This was where your mum came in. She wants the best for you, always has, but that day she couldn't see beyond that shithouse actor.

We all want this to work out well, she told them. And we're so excited about Garvey Quinn.

This was when you knew they had her. You saw the angry one's face go even blacker.

Mr Quinn's participation could not be guaranteed if there was any fear that his position would be compromised by public appearances by your son.

Your mum looked shocked by this, but she smiled her hardest.

Don't worry, Bryan's not going anywhere, are you love? You're happy right here.

But the bottom line is, we've got to have that in writing.

Then a contract was pushed in front of you. It should be fine, because that's all you've ever wanted in the years since everything went down the drain, just not to be noticed by the world, but on their terms it didn't seem right. You hesitated, until the angry one gave up waiting.

The bottom line, mate, is that when you tricked the world into thinking you were dead, you committed a criminal act, for which charges could still be brought. And without our legal protection that's just what will happen, so are you going to sign or not?

So of course you did sign, and they went away, and you thought, well, just accept everything, what else is there to do? That is until that director and the other two finally came to see you. With them in here talking like you wouldn't exist if they hadn't thought of you, it was like it wasn't your life anymore. When you were in the public eye, that was different, no matter how many stories they printed, how many TV shows you were on, even when they started showing you really fucking everything up, it was only ever you up there. You might have hated it, but it was you and you alone. But when you find yourself turning into a story, then it's not you anymore. It's just another freak doing stupid stuff, and why would anybody want to know?

After you shout, your mum looks like she's had the stuffing knocked out of her, and you say sorry, and she says, that's all right son. But you know it's not really. You watch her, nothing to do, no point now, can't go out getting things for you, so you finally say, almost without thinking, it's all right Mum, you can go home now, I'll be all right. She'd rented out the house I'd bought her with the money from my first Uncle Tobys endorsement, and she can get the place back, and you see her look pleased at the idea. You know, and she knows, that's something's going to be different now, and though you don't know what it is, you know you've got to be alone to deal with it, like you used to be alone in the pool. That's about the one thing you still remember about the pool, the being alone.

Mum's not supposed to show her face outside either, in case she's recognised and the trail leads back to me, but she gets away surprisingly easily, even books a flight under her own name without any problems. Maybe without me around, she's just not all that recognisable.

Once she's gone, you settle back in, with everything that's ever happened now back in full glare in front of you like never before, which is just what they would have liked you to talk about, but you wouldn't give them that satisfaction, not ever, not them. You used to keep it away, keep the blind down through eating, drinking, sleeping, but from now on you hardly ever sleep, you don't drink, and all the KFC and the pizzas and the barbecue chooks just mount up in a big pile. Maybe you pick at a nugget as you go by sometimes, but most of the time you can hardly bear to look at it, you've got more important things on your mind now, and the stuff ends up going down the garbage chute, which is probably where some people think you should have gone.

★ ★ ★

GaRVEY QUiNN

The biggest worry now is that I'm putting on so much weight so fast that they won't get through shooting what they call the medium-chubby scenes in time before I blow out to stage three. I'm supposed to still look like an athlete who's got slack and packed it on a bit, not a really fat guy who gets stuck in doorways. Dr Roland Gussett's been adjusting my diet to try to slow me down a bit, a few less eggs at breakfast, a few less pork spare ribs at lunch, some different tablets to alter the absorption rate, but it's a losing battle. The trouble is, these adjustments make me so deperately hungry I have to cheat. When the cook leaves after breakfast I cook myself some extra eggs, bacon, sausages, thick white toast, and I pile on the butter. At lunch, on the set, after I've finished what they've cooked for me, I knock over the stack of thick mustardy ham sandwiches I've smuggled in, though it never seems nearly enough.

Dinner though, is not a problem. Once the chef leaves, I've got the whole evening ahead of me to just cook and cook and cook. I'm getting quite good at it, too, starting to experiment a bit. Fried bread sautéed in goose fat has become a special favourite of mine. Madeleine eats all her meals out on the balcony now, whatever the weather, that's when she's home, perched on the little wrought iron outdoor chair with her hair blowing in the wind, drying it after the last swim.

StUffED

She seems to eat out a lot more than before, often going out to dinner with her theatre pals who take her to health food restaurants, looking after her as if she's going through some ordeal, which I consider a bit unfair to me, considering the circumstances. Not that she ever says anything.

Back on the set, they've started calling me tubby, which pisses me off no end. When I walk in in the morning it's, hi ya tubby, how's it going tubby, and people come over and pinch me on the gut or the bum to see how it's progressing, or tickle me under the chin, where I'm developing quite a roll. Today is the worst yet, because I'm back in the pool, in my Speedos, with it all hanging out. It's my last swimming scene, the Olympic selection trials, and everybody knows I haven't got a hope in hell, even though I'm still the record holder. We start off filming at the warm-up pool where I'm doing a few laps, still hoping I can psyche myself up into a such a huge effort that I'll overcome my lack of condition. But when I step out, Arthur Snow's standing there, holding a stopwatch, he's been timing me even though he's no longer my coach. Duncan Young, as Arthur, seems to really enjoy the scenes where I'm in deep shit.

You fat, useless piece of lard, he gets to shout at me. It's a wonder you can even float anymore.

I turn to walk away. You're not my coach anymore, Arthur. But he comes after me, pointing at my gut.

You know what I see when I see that?

My stomach, what do you think?

What I see, Bryan, is the thousands upon thousands of laps you swam for me. Every lap you ever swam, from when you came to me at twelve, those laps with me willing you every inch of the way, my whole emotional life invested in finding that extra something that would take you to greatness.

I was swimming for me, not for you.

GarVEY QUiNN

What about the thousands of little kids, and all their mums and dads, the ones who worshipped you, the role model who proved to them that perfection was possible? They'll see you swim today and they'll feel sick to the stomach with disappointment, that this is what it can come to.

Leave me alone! I'm going to swim.

Pull out. Fake an injury. Don't disgrace yourself one more time.

Then I turn, angrily, and just for that moment, the old fire is back in my eyes.

I'm going to swim. Do you think I don't know how much this means to people? I'm going to find something extra, for them and for me.

I walk away, but then I turn back to Arthur.

And for you.

Of course I don't find something extra. The race is a heat, and all I need is fourth place to get into the semis, but to the Bryan of old, fourth would have been unthinkable. The race scene, filmed with just a swimmer each side of me, to be cut into actual Olympic trial footage later on, sees me floundering along at the back. My graceful one two three four breathe style leaves me, I stick my head up too often to gasp for air, and when I touch in at the end, long after the rest, I lean against the end of the pool, hanging my head in shame, the other swimmers refusing to look at me.

Then comes the long walk, the walk of shame. So dejected I can't even think to cover my flab with a tracksuit, I have to walk right round the pool to get to the change rooms, in front of a hushed, despondent crowd. The next event is the women's 200 butterfly final, and Vicki, to everyone's surprise, has qualified fastest, finding herself suddenly at the point of stepping up from contender to champion. The line of women swimmers comes towards me on their way to the blocks, as I trudge along with my head down. Madeleine, as Vicki, is last in line, and with her tracksuit off, looks sleeker and more perfect than ever before. It crosses my mind that, as was the case with Bryan and Vicki in the script, we haven't made love for weeks, haven't even kissed. I've been too busy eating.

As Madeleine and I pass each other, I have to look up, and pause for just a moment, and give her a look of pain and sorrow. Seagrave has told me the look has to say, I'm sorry Vicki, but I don't know how you can be that exact about what you do with your eyes, whatever acting coaches tell you, and I've always found that emotional stuff a bit out of reach. Madeleine has to look my way for just a split second, as if she's taking this in, but then look away quickly as if she's working hard to keep her emotions together for the race. As she walks away, though, a tear trickles down her face. Seagrave offered her glycerine but Madeleine refused it, saying she's a good enough actor to make a tear come without any artificial assistance. What she does certainly looks real enough to me.

Then I walk on, to the change room, but stay in the doorway so I can peek out and watch Madeleine's race. She wins, brilliantly, and the crowd goes wild, as if they really need someone to cheer for after the way I've dashed their hopes. So she's off to the Olympics as a gold medal favourite, but I'm out of the place, throwing my tracksuit on without bothering to shower, and sneaking out a side entrance with the help of a sad-faced official who says, bad luck, son, you were real good in your day. Next time I'm seen I'm sitting in a takeaway, chomping on a kebab and bawling my eyes out while the bewildered Lebanese proprietors look on from the kitchen doorway. Interestingly, when we film the scene, it turns out I don't need any glycerine either, as soon as I think of Madelaine the tears come pouring out, but maybe that just means I'm a better actor than I thought. I get it right in one take, and when it's over, Seagrave shouts bravo and gives me a hug, the first time that's ever happened.

For most of the rest of the filming, thankfully, I get to keep my clothes on. Because of the worries about how fast my weight was ballooning out, they got the final disastrous pool sequence out of the way while it was still just possible to believe that I might actually make it from one end to the other. With that done, we go back to doing some scenes that really take place earlier in the story, but with my gear on the disparity in my weight between one scene and another isn't going to be too obvious, so they tell me. I take to wearing really loose floppy shirts, the same way that Bryan Mars apparently was doing by then. I remember people started calling him the swimming tent.

We go back to the time not so long after the rescue when Bryan, already a champion, is now a hero as well. Everybody wants a piece of him, he's on every show, in every magazine, endorsing this that and the other, he just can't say no. And especially he can't say no to food. He gets invited to party after party, really top class ones and mostly he accepts. Girls throw themselves over him, but he's faithful to Vicki, who's gone to train up in Queensland with a new coach, after Arthur Snow kicked her out of his squad. So at these parties, instead of hiving off to the bedroom with every chick who tells him how wonderful he is and flashes her headlights at him, he gets stuck into the food. Like I said, these parties are big time stuff, so the food's fantastic, and there's heaps of it. And he knows he shouldn't, because of his training routine, but he just can't stop himself pigging out.

So in this scene, at a big bash that's being turned on for the launch of a new fashion magazine, he finds himself bored shitless by the speeches and the kissing and the hullo darling you look fabulous, and while all the others are watching some stupid presentation, he sets himself up beside this enormous table loaded with food. He picks up a whole tray of satay chicken wings, and he's happily chomping away at that. All these waiters who've been hired for the night keep coming by offering him other stuff when he's already got his hands full and just trying to get on with eating, and with his mouth full of chicken wing he keeps having to say, I'm all right thanks, thanks, I'm fine. Eventually, when it's happened once too often, he notices that behind a curtain there's a little alcove with nothing going on in it. So he scoops up three or four trays, some nice big pink prawns with a garlic dip, more chicken, a big plate of blue cheese and runny camembert and some fantastic goose liver pâté and chunks of Turkish bread, and sets himself up in the alcove. There's no table or chair or anything, so he sits down on the floor and pulls this curtain over a bit, and really starts stuffing himself.

Next thing you know, a photographer looks in and sees this champion, this hero, making a complete slob of himself, and starts clicking away. I have to leap up, and the couple of trays I've got balanced on my lap go flying. The photographer gets a shot of this, too, me with the dip for the prawns now splashed all over my shirt, and food spilling out of my mouth as I shout, don't you fucking dare! I have to chase the photographer across the room, bumping into all these fashion types who spill champagne down their cleavages, and then when he disppears into the lift, I head down the fire escape and meet him at the bottom. I start whacking into him, trying to get the camera off him, but there're two other photographers there, and they photograph what's going on. I nearly get the camera off the first photographer, but then a couple of security guards come charging up and grab hold of me. As they drag me out of the lobby, off the premises, with a whole lot of ritzy hotel guests looking on, I shout, I'm Bryan Mars, don't you realise, I'm Bryan Mars!

Then they do some shots of me at the flat, reacting to the newspapers in the morning after a lonely, sleepless night spent tossing and turning. Two of the newspapers have photos, one shows me leaping up and spilling food all over the place, the other has the attack on the photographer. There are headlines like, Hero bites off more than he can chew, and, New Olympic event – the food fight. I try to ring Vicki, looking at her photograph while I'm dialling just to make sure the audience gets the point. She doesn't answer, but then the phone starts running hot, with the media on my back, and I have to keep shouting things like, no comment, bugger off. Then my manager rings and says, that could have cost you a million bucks. Finally I take the phone off the hook, and start cooking some eggs for comfort. They've let me choose the ingredients myself for this scene, and I make a big runny omelette with plenty of cheese, naturally cooked in goose fat. That's the end of the scene, the cooking, and they have to stop me eating the omelette so they can get the set ready for the next scene, Vicki's unexpected arrival. It just seems such a shame to waste good food like that.

Vicki and Bryan at this stage haven't actually split, they've just been separated by her move to train interstate. So while Bryan's lying back gloomily munching Tim Tams and channel surfing the kids' cartoons, Vicki lets herself in. She still has her own key. I have to say, Vicki!, like everybody doesn't already know what her name is. Then Madeleine has to say to me, I've been trying to phone you all day, before I left home, from the airport in Brisbane, then from the airport here. I've been worried sick, I thought you must have done something terrible. I explain about the media, and the phone off the hook, and all that. And she tells me, it's breaking my heart, what's happening to you, I wish to God you'd never stepped on that boat. And I say, me too, if only I could go back to when things were simple, when all I had to do was swim. And she says, Bryan, you can still have that, I believe in you. She kisses me, and I push the Tim Tams packet aside and stand up, and let her lead me into the bedroom.

This love scene is shot differently from the earlier ones, much more discreetly, at least in terms of how much of me is shown. As Seagrave said, who wants to watch flab rooting? Madeleine has to take everything off again, and boogie around on top of me, but most of me stays obscured by the sheet, which the costume lady comes and fiddles with now and again whenever there's a danger of too much of me poking through. The idea is that Vicki is trying her hardest to bring back the old magic, perhaps even trying too hard. Seagrave's told her to look desperate, while I have to look like I already know it's all hopeless. Eventually we give up, and lie silently next to each other, a tear trickling down Madeleine's face. Again, she does it without glycerine. I drift off to sleep, and when I wake, she's gone and so is her bag. I open the fridge.

There are a few more of these decline scenes. These, of course, actually take place before the big pool scene we've already shot, the debacle at the Olympic trials, which was rushed through production before I got too porky. In one I'm wandering the streets, lonely and dejected as hell, when I'm recognised by some friendly sports fans outside a pub, who want me to know how much they're on my side. Don't let the bastards get you mate, they tell me, it's the tall poppy syndrome at work, look what they did to Dawnie Fraser and Phar Lap. Look at how much shit they pour on Greg Norman. I fall in with them, and wind up at a night club in the early hours, and when some loudmouth starts giving me a hard time, I take a swing at him. He swings back, shouting you're history now, Mars, you're fucked, and it turns into an all-in brawl, with blood everywhere. I spend what's left of the night in a cell with a bunch of drunks and sleazos, and I'm in the papers again, headlines like, A champion's shame, Superfish goes belly-up, and The wild life of Bryan. I'm on TV, too, caught as I run from the cop shop to my manager's car. He tells me, there's not much more I can do for you, Bryan. I hang my head in shame, which is something I'm having to do a lot.

After this there's a bit of a break while I pack on more weight for the scenes at the Olympics. Now nobody cares how much I eat, the more the better, so I can stop all the secrecy and eat anything, anytime. In just a couple of weeks I'm really ballooning, and everybody seems really pleased with me. Whenever Roland Gussett comes to check on me he smiles and pats me on the back, saying things like, way to go, and what a champ, especially when I've just got off the scales. I'm feeling sort of proud, too, in a weird sort of way, like I'm doing a job well. It's become a fulltime thing now, eating food, cooking food, thinking about food, and I even dream about food. It's funny, sometimes, how at a particular time in your life something like this can completely take you over, not leave room for worrying about anything else, as if your body's looking after you, it knows what you need. Which I suppose is what happened to Bryan Mars, too, when the going got tough. I'm even starting to understand some of that acting talk that used to piss me off so much before, about finding the central truth of a character, taking the same journey. Sometimes, as I take the first bite of a wheel of deep-fried camembert, I think I am Bryan Mars.

Then something happens that I never even imagined was

possible. One morning, the cook's just left, I've had a great breakfast, and I'm lying back wondering whether I might just finish things off with some more fried bread, when Madeleine comes in off the balcony, where's she's been taking a long time over her muesli. In fact she was already sitting out there with it when I first got up, before the cook had even arrived. She stands staring at me, like she's sizing me up, and I've got to admit, I probably don't look my best. Mostly when Madeleine's around these days I wear something loose and floppy, even in bed, but this time I'm just in a pair of footy shorts, some new, bigger ones. I've taken my shirt off because I was feeling so full, and a new batch of larger shirts hasn't arrived yet. And Madeleine says, Garvey, I want you to know I really respect what you're doing.

Thanks, I say.

This sort of dedication to a part is something special. Not many actors would be brave enough to do this to themselves, to desecrate their own body like this.

No. I suppose they wouldn't.

But. And maybe this is the price you have to pay for great art. I'm feeling crowded out by what you're doing. I don't feel you're leaving me any space.

Space? I look down at my stomach, and see the way I'm spreading out over the chair, but I think she's probably talking about something more emotional, the way women tend to.

And I feel that until all this is over, I have to be by myself, she says. Until you're back to your old self again and we can be together like we were.

Madeleine, I wouldn't have done this without you, I tell her. I wouldn't have had the courage. And if you go, I don't know how I'll get through the rest of it.

Sorry, she says. I've hardly got enough courage left to get myself through this.

GarVeY QUiNN

There's nothing more I can say. Madeleine goes into the bedroom and starts packing, and I decide that I will have that fried bread. As I eat it, I again find myself thinking about how Bryan Mars must have felt. It's amazing at a time like this, how much eating can take the pain away, take the edge off it at least, and I add some Spanish sausages, some ham and some bacon, and I start to realise it's not so long until lunch.

I hardly see Madeleine again after this, as we don't have any more dialogue together, just some glances beside the pool at the Olympics, me transfixed, her averting her eyes. Bryan's manager had washed his hands of him, and taken on a couple of hot new kids, but then somehow lined up Bryan a gig as a commentator at the Olympics. Even though he's in disgrace, he knows a lot about swimming, and he's always been pretty good on screen, in interviews and such, looked on as a potential TV personality once his swimming days are over. Not that that's likely to happen now, but Alexander Morton has a big stake in the channel, and he still feels some loyalty.

But now that his swimming days are over, he's a dead loss. Wardrobe have given me this stupid commentator's blazer, bright purple, and they've made it deliberately much too tight to emphasise how fat I've become. The other commentators in the box are all lean and stylish, and like the people on the set, they're calling me tubby, so I know how Bryan must have felt. What's worse, the gift of the gab seems to go.

Good turn there from, um, Robin, um, er Robertson, no, it is Robinson, and about, what, say half a length behind, here comes Kilpatrick from Scotland. Or maybe that should be Ireland, look I'll check on that in a minute. And Czerp, um Czerpol, um, something, the Polish swimmer, anyway, is pretty close too, so it's all getting really exciting in the men's 100 butterfly final.

Thank you Bryan, actually we're in the middle of the

medley relay. After those expert comments from Bryan Mars, we'll let Ted Gibbs take us through to end.

Thanks mate, just to avoid any confusion, it's Kilpatrick from the US, then Roberts, then Czerpinski from the Czech Republic.

After a couple more fiascos like that, Bryan gets taken off actual race commentaries and given little expert opinion spots between races.

Bryan, Herman Schell would know that he must have a real shot at the world record tonight, that record that's stood for so many years, and which he's said is the one thing in swimming he still wants. And yet there's a gold medal at stake here, too, isn't there Bryan?, so maybe you can tell us, what must be going on in his head right now. How does a swimmer balance that, wanting that record so much, yet knowing that if he really goes out there and puts it on the line, if he gets those split times wrong, he could end up with silver, or worse. You've been there, Bryan, in the Commonwealth Games anyway, so run us through it.

Well, yeah, it is sort of hard. I mean, a world record's one thing. But then, a gold medal's another thing. They're two different things, in fact, you could really say. And if Herman Snell …

It's Schell, Bryan.

Yeah, Schell, sorry, that's what I meant. If he really wants the world record, well, I suppose he'll have a go at it. But on the other hand, um, if he wants the gold medal. Well, I suppose that's what he'll go for instead.

Of course, if he gets the world record, there's a good chance he'll end up with the gold as well.

Yeah, that's true, that's a good way of looking at it. Thanks.

Thank you Bryan Mars. More expert comments from

Bryan Mars later on.

But not many more. After a couple more fiascos, the other sportscasters virtually go on strike to get him out of the commentary box. Alexander Morton, though, still isn't prepared to cut him adrift, because after all, Bryan saved his life. So as a last resort, Bryan gets given the job of doing interviews down by the pool, fronting up to swimmers straight after a race, how do you feel, when did you know you had it in the bag, that sort of thing. This doesn't go nearly as badly, because the swimmers do most of the talking, they're so pumped up after winning. I have to do little smiles and nods, and when one of them says, I'll tell you mate, there's nothing in this world so exciting as winning an Olympic gold, I have to give this long wistful look as he walks off. You're supposed to be able to see me thinking about what I've let slip away. Wistful looks are actually quite hard to do, because mostly you just end up looking like a moron.

But then come the two really big moments at the Games. In the first one Vicki Michaels has won, brilliantly, and as Madeleine steps from the pool, accepts congratulations from the others, towels herself off, and then starts walking towards the interview spot, I have to start shaking, make the microphone sort of vibrate in my hand, I'm that nervous. Then she starts running towards me with this huge joyous smile, and I give a little smile back, what's supposed to be a smile of hope. She's got her arms outstretched, like she's about to give me this huge hug, and I push the microphone forward a bit, and mumble, Vicki. But she runs straight past, like she doesn't even see me, and I turn to see her leap into the arms of this enormous guy in a Swedish team uniform. She's still just got her swimmers on, and she wraps her legs around his waist, and he puts his hand on her bum, and they kiss and kiss and kiss. That's when I have to do another wistful look as I walk away, and somehow I think that wistful look goes pretty well.

Now we're really getting down to business. I go back to my food trailer and have a really big lunch, including a whole leg of lamb with rosemary and that nice pudding they make from the fat that comes off it. Then I have to do a scene where Bryan has lunch, the lunch he has straight after Vicki's big win, sitting alone in a corner of the press dining room, a whole table of food to himself, shunned and sniggered at by the media professionals. So I get to eat that lunch as well, prawns and barbecue pork ribs, and there's plenty of it because they're set up to do a lot of takes if necessary. As it turns out I get it in one go, they just set the cameras rolling and I just eat and eat and eat until there's nothing left on the table, I'm hardly even aware that there's anybody watching me. Afterwards Seagrave tells me what a fantastic job I'm doing, I always knew you were Oscar material, he says.

For special effects, I hear him say to someone as he walks away afterwards.

So, full of all this food, I go into the scene where I do my last interview. This is meant to be the most painful of all because I'm interviewing this young kid, Danny Visser, who Arthur Snow took onto his squad after he kicked me out. Danny's won the gold, though he didn't get anywhere near the world record, which I still hold, but he's cocky as hell.

Great swim Danny, how do you feel?

Like I'm king of the world, mate. This is just incredible.

So what next, Danny?

Now that I've got the gold out of the way, I'm going to kick the crap out of that world record. There's no room for a fat has-been in the record books.

Yeah, well, thanks a lot, Danny.

But he keeps talking. Before I go, I want to thank my coach Arthur Snow. Arthur had faith in me because he knew I'd put in the work, keep my mind on swimming and not flush my career down the toilet. Arthur's had some big disappointments, but I hope I've helped him get back his faith in human nature. Good on you Bryan.

Then he has to slap me on the back as he goes, and I topple backwards into the pool. This brings laughter at first, but then I go under, come up struggling and gasping, then go under again. My instructions are to come up a third time, and then when I go under after that, Danny Visser will leap in and rescue me. After all that lunch, though, I can't even make it back up for a third time. This is even worse than in the shark tank. As I try and hold onto my last breath, I realise Danny Visser must be waiting and waiting for his cue, my third appearance and disappearance, before he does anything. Somebody must prod him into action eventually, but by the time he jumps in and grabs me, I'm completely helpless, gone. Danny brings me to the side of the pool, where other hands reach down to pull me onto the deck, and I hear someone say, shit the bastard's heavy. I'm meant to just lie there, exhausted and stunned, and as people realise that I'm all right, they walk away, one by one, until I'm stretched out there all alone. I keep lying there, just staring at the sky, until someone calls out, you can get up now, Garvey, we're finished for the day, but I don't feel I can, I just stay there until eventually a couple of gaffers come and move me because I'm in the way of a cable.

I have to take a couple of days off, I'm so shattered by it all. The cook comes along with an assistant, and they stay around the flat all day. I just lie in bed, and food keeps appearing, and I keep eating it until they knock off late at night, when they think I'm ready to go to sleep. I drift off as I lie there wondering whether I have enough strength to get up and see what's in the fridge.

Fortunately the remaining scenes don't take much acting, hardly any lines to remember, mostly just sitting looking dejected in an airline seat, plus a bit of shuffling around. Flying home in disgrace, I just sit and stare at the seat in front of me while other passengers sneak looks as they come and go up and down the aisle. I'm meant to look like I'm thinking a lot, mulling something over. Then I do an airport arrival scene, stepping out into a grey drizzly dawn, all alone in the world, when I could have had everything. But then Mum steps out of the shadows, played by Sandra-Lee Butcher, this old chain-smoking boot who was the matron in the first series of *Medical Emergency*.

I still believe in you, son, no matter what anybody else says.

Sorry Mum. Right now I have to be alone. It's best for everybody. And I walk away, while Mum sheds a tear. Sandra-Lee Butcher doesn't hold back on the glycerine.

The producers are pleased they got real rain for the airport scene, and they rush to get the final beach scene done while the weather's still wet. Seagrave says, rain always makes a suicide feel so much more authentic. All I have to do is step out of my car, the roomy old Landcruiser that's replaced Bryan's squeezy little BMW M3, slog down through the sandhills, stare out to sea, drop my gear, and head out into the waves. I've asked Seagrave, am I trying to kill myself, or just disappear, but all he'll tell me is, you don't know, and neither should the audience. Not that being told one way or the other would have made much difference to how I played it, but Madeleine always told me actors are supposed ask those sort of questions.

Next time there's a sunny day, they pick me up and drive

to a little cove at a different beach. I have to get my gear off yet again and lie on my back, stock still in the very edge of the surf, my eyes closed like I'm unconscious. They have me lying there starkers, my flab and my tackle on display, but then they stuff around for ages over some problem with a camera, and nobody bothers to come and throw a blanket over me or anything. There's a high sandhill behind, and there's a ring of people up there rubbernecking the way they always do when there's a movie being made, and I can see these boofheads from the surf club sniggering. I just want them to get it over with so I can go home and eat, and try to remember what dignity feels like.

At last, when the problem's fixed, I do the wake-up scene, gradually coming round, looking up at the sky, realising I'm still alive. Think of Robinson Crusoe, Seagrave says, like that's supposed to be a help. When I get the strength to prop myself up, I look out to sea, and way way out there's a surfboard rider, unusually, a big fat one. Then on the beach I spot what must be his pile of gear, there's nobody else around, and I run to it as best I can, hunched over, bare arsed, as ridiculous as anything, but that's how Seagrave wants it. And in someone else's clothes, I leave the beach, ready to begin my life in hiding. Cut.

With no more filming for months, nothing but eating ahead of me, I hoped Seagrave at least might have come up and said something like, thanks for all your hard work, I know it's been tough, but not a word. The last I see of him that day is when he's heading for his car, over by the surf club, and he doesn't even look back, like he couldn't give a shit. This time he's driving a bright yellow Bentley Turbo convertible with the top down even though it's raining, and as he does a wheelie coming out of the carpark, his big Stetson hat blows off, the first time it's come off all day. He's got

StUffED

a two-inch stripe of stubble down the middle of his head, like a stunted Mohawk.

★ ★ ★

BRYAN MARS

You read the note that's been stuck under the door. You've heard the phone ring a few times but you don't bother answering it, you don't want to hear anything from anyone who's got anything to do with you being here, and who else would have been ringing but the head of security? Now he's left you this note that says, people in the floor below are complaining to the management, they say it feels like there's a herd of elephants up there. Whatever it is you're doing, will you please stop it immediately or we won't be able to guarantee your security.

You tear up the note. Bastards. Supposed to be looking after your every need, but they're at you for one thing after another. First you get the note that the garbage disposal can't cope with the extreme amounts of food being thrown down it, could you please continue eating the agreed amount. You'll eat what you fucking well like, so you ignore them, and after a while the deliveries are cut down. It's the stuff with the fat in it that sickens you most, and the heavy juicy meat, and the sugar and the cream, you can hardly bear to think about it anymore, let alone have it around the place. You even throw a new giant supersize pizza right over the balcony, still in its box, when it's arrived just after you've had your apple for the day and you find the pizza is too big to fit down the chute. They leave notes about that too, any more such indiscreet acts and your protection from prosecution can no longer be guaranteed. Which is bullshit, because you know there's no way they're going to let you out of here until the movie comes out, and then they're going to trot you out like a circus freak, probably a double act with you and that awful actor. I wouldn't trust that lot as far as I could throw them.

You get other aggravation, too, for spending so much time out on the balcony, leaning over to look at the people down below when you're not jogging up and down it. The note tells you, as an extremely conspicuous figure, you appear to be deliberately undermining the efforts being made to keep you out of public view. Measures that are being taken in your own best interests. If we can't depend on your co-operation, more drastic measures may have to be taken. Which is even more bullshit. What measures can anyone take against you now? This is when you get so angry that you step up the jogging, you make sure your feet hit the ground harder, now that you're starting to work up just a tiny bit of kneelift. That's when the note about the vibration comes, and you make your feet hit harder still.

A day later, you hear noises underneath, bumping and banging like furniture, and then you look down over the balcony to the street. You see a removal van, furniture being put into it, and you know what's happened, they're moving the people out because they know they won't stop you. You pump your arms in the air, yes, you shout, and then you find something's coming over you, your skin's tingling and you're remembering some moment from somewhere far off, you're in a pool, and people are shouting, you're pumping your arms then, too, and you wonder, is this where you want to go, or do you just want to go in and eat some more? Wouldn't that be better for everyone now?

You go back in. You sit, you flop down, like you used to.

There's food there, some barbecue pork ribs, and you reach, but somehow you can't touch it, but you can't get up again either, suddenly there's that heavy feeling again, holding you down. You reach for the remote, flick the TV on, hoping for something that will hold back the torrent of images that's looming up in your head. There's a nature show, leaping dolphins, but right away it's got you feeling water all around you, whooshing over your skin, you're wanting to go one two three four breathe, and you have to flick the channel because of where that will take you. You lock onto a night football match, that's all right, you don't care about football, don't know about it, it's just a pattern, little figures zigging and zagging across a field of meaningless lines, again and again, action, but nothing happening, just as long as nothing happens.

But a figure bursts out of the pattern. He's crashed through a line of others with the ball under his arm, he's put it over a line and the crowd's roaring, wave after wave of shouting, all for him, and you feel what he's feeling, lifted up in the air, like when you got that world record.

You flick over to a crime show. You're watching some kind of detective, he's following somebody into a bar. They talk, someone's hitting him from behind, but he turns, his fist goes in hard, you feel it hit bone, you feel the blood on your knuckles, and you see the fist coming back at you, you hear the words, you're history now, Mars, you're fucked, and you know it's true, you still are.

But here's something, you change channels again and this is what you want, it's some award, showbiz by the look of it, people all dressed up, sitting in an audience, then called up on stage, the envelope please, and the winner is, and then tears and hugs and kisses, and none of it means anything, it's for shows about nothing, people on about nothing, nothing except themselves, I just loved playing that part because it was so real, I want to thank the director for believing in me, hey, is this really happening to me, thank God for giving me the strength to be here tonight, we all just have to follow our dreams, and on they go, on and on and on. And you start to feel better, it's softening again, the edges are blurring.

And then, now to present the award for best supporting actress, someone we all remember for his fine work in *Medical Emergency*, but about to be seen in the soon to be released feature that everybody's talking about, *Fish Out of Water*. Welcome Garvey Quinn. And there he is, walking on with a stupid grin, and he's fat! He's fat! He's too fat for his suit, he looks like a blimp, and they must have done it on purpose, they knew all along what they were going to do. And what's worse, Mum trusted them completely, and you even did a bit, because you never could have imagined anybody could go quite that far!

So now you know exactly what they're doing to you. Your legs make you stand up as he reaches the dais and says, I don't always look like this, and gets a laugh. Then he says, like he's trying to be a stand-up comic, a funny thing happened to me on the way here tonight. The police pulled over the truck I was in and gave the driver a ticket. They said he should have had a sign saying, caution, wide load. You can't believe it, this gets a laugh too. You hear more stupid stuff and then he rips the envelope open, but fortunately all he says is somebody's name, another name that means nothing, and somebody running up, and kisses all round, and thanks to my mum who always believed I could do it, and then they're going off, so at least you won't have to see him any more for now. But he hasn't gone, he's just standing there, they show the actress run down and start kissing some bloke, and then you see him, wobbling over to the edge of the stage like he's completely lost it. And as you watch it all happening, you can hear yourself, as if you're listening from a distance, you hear yourself going Aaaaarrrghh!!!

★ ★ ★

GaRvEY QUiNN

A few weeks after filming's finally over, my agent Stuie Fengler talks me into doing something really stupid. I don't go out at all these days, the only time I've been anywhere for months was to the studio to film the Darwin house scenes, and then to the sound studio to do the voice-overs. A limo came and got me then, a stretch limo with extra wide rear doors, but even that didn't make it easy, so I prefer to stay where I am, just as long as the food keeps coming. But Stuie's been getting pressure from the publicity people, trying to whip up interest in the movie. They tell him, your client's just not pulling his weight, hah-hah. It seems there's a clause in the contract obliging me to do certain things in the interests of promotion, and I risk being sued. So Stuie turns up, really in a lather about it.

Garvey, just because the character you're playing hid from the world, doesn't mean you have to. You've got to keep in mind, there's life for you after *Fish Out of Water*. Do you want to make yourself unemployable?

I don't know, I say, but he doesn't seem to hear, just pushes on.

Now, off my own bat, I've talked the AFI organiser into letting you present an award. Any actor who wants to keep his profile up in the business would kill for a chance like this.

I'm not just any actor.

Listen sunshine, this is your first feature and it hasn't even been released yet. Grow up and get off your fat bum! Then he seems to realise what he's said. Sorry, I know you're not fat because you enjoy it.

I'm not sure whether I agree, so I don't say anything.

The reality is, if you don't accept this opportunity, you, and I, are likely to find ourselves dealing with some heavy legal shit. That's the, er, bottom line.

Looking back, the heavy legal shit might have been better, even for poor Stuie. He didn't come out of it too well either, with the organisers blaming him for putting me up in the first place, and saying they'd never accept another of his clients again, that I was a disgrace to the profession, which I suppose I am. Anyway, I agreed to do it, and soon afterwards an enormous dinner suit was flown over from the States, apparently made by Marlon Brando's tailor, so I suppose I should have felt honoured.

I don't try to get the dinner suit on until the day of the awards, and I find that even though it's big, it's not quite big enough. To get the trousers on I have to lie on the bed, and roll each trouser leg up, stick my foot in it, then roll it down again. It's so tight fitting it's a bit like putting your dick into a condom, though not nearly that easy or with as much hope of enjoyment. I keep getting stuck halfway, and when, after about half an hour, I've finally got the legs sorted out, then I have to squeeze my bum into it. I tug and tug and nothing happens, and I'm sweating and breathing heavily and ready to give up, but then suddenly something seems to give way, and I'm in the trousers, it's all right. I stand up, but then I find the reason it got easier was that I've ripped the seat right open. That's when the buzzer rings, it's the limousine that's been sent to take me to the awards, and when Stuie and the driver come up, they're pissed off that I'm not nearly ready. They help me into the shirt and the jacket, one pushing, one pulling, and tie my shoes up for me because it's hard to reach down to do it myself. These days, with Madeleine not around, I've gone back to wearing thongs, which make a lot of sense.

In the limo I'm still trying to learn this stupid script that they've had written for me, the patter. The idea is to show how comfortable I am with what I've done to myself, remind people that I'm an actor playing a role, not a hopeless lardguts. Just keep it light, tell them, I'm not usually like this, and give a little laugh, and wait for them to laugh back, sympathetically, because it's mostly an industry audience, and they appreciate this sort of professional dedication. Then I have to do this stupid joke about coming there in a truck, and it not having a wide load sign, and then, Marlon Brando sends his apologies, he couldn't be here tonight, but he did send his suit along. Somebody actually got paid for writing that.

I hate doing that sort of stand-up stuff, the idea of it makes me nervous as hell, and things don't get any better when I arrive at the awards, because there are all the people in the world I least want to see, and there's no way I can hide from them, not looking like I do. First off the rank is Johnny Hearn. He was the one in Seagrave's last film, playing the demented mass murderer, but he was just considered too plain looking, too downright ugly, to play golden boy Bryan Mars. Now when I see him at the awards he's positively glowing, and what's more he doesn't look nearly so ugly. He's leaner, more muscular than before, like he's been working out, and somehow it even seems to have improved the proportions of his face. He'd have looked good as Bryan Mars, the old Bryan Mars, anyway.

When Johnny Hearn sees me he does this big, over the top reaction, standing there gobsmacked, as if he's trying to take in what he's just seen. Then he says, Jesus H. Christ! Garvey, you poor bastard.

How you going, Johnny?, is all I can say.

Great. Just great. Never been better. What a lucky escape, huh?

What was?

I had one more go at trying to persuade Stirling to let me play Bryan Mars, but the same day he signed you up. I was shattered. I was an emotional wreck. I was ready to walk away from the business. But you know what happened? The very next day I got the call. I mean THE call. Hollywood wanted me. Tarantino. Jesus Christ, I still shudder to think about it, if Stirling had said yes, I would have been stuck here, would have had to knock back Quentin, and what's more I would have had to do this to myself.

It's pretty obvious what doing this to myself means, because as he says it he's looking at my stomach. What's worse he's trying to act as if he cares. He's a good actor, but not that good.

I feel for you, man. To be honest, I think Stirling's gone completely crazy.

Has he?

Well, for fuck sake, first of all turning it into a porn flick, and then imagining audiences will want to watch a hero who looks like, well, you know …

He doesn't get to finish describing what I look like, because other people want his company, Johnny, mate, shit you're looking good.

Got to go, Garvey, everybody wants a piece of me. This is just a flying visit, I came over because my girlfriend's up for an award, best supporting actress.

Oh, that's the one I'm presenting, what's her … But he's gone. I turn round, and notice someone smirking at my trousers, and then there's Austin Irwin.

Garvey, what a surprise.

Hullo Austin.

Think you can stay awake through this one?

I have trouble working out what he's on about, until I remember the play, with him and Madeleine in it, Madeleine's bum, way back when all this had just started. There's not much to say to a question like that.

I should be all right.

Fortunately I won't be around to see. Just dropped in for a few quick hellos, but I have to dash off to the Opera House.

Oh, is there something good on?

Me. I'm in *Hamlet*. I am Hamlet. If I win they'll cross to me live in the dressing room at interval.

Well, good luck, anyway.

Yes. Had a big phone bill so I took a guest role in this unspeakable medical soap, you might have heard of it, it's called *Medical Emergency*.

But …

They were going to axe it but then they decided all it needed was a change of cast, it's amazing what a bit of real acting talent can do for a show that seems to be on its last legs. Anyway, I did such a good job they put me up for a gong. Be seeing you, Garvey, bit hard not to, isn't it? Oh, and if you see Madeleine, wish her good luck for me.

Oh, is she …

Then we're called to our places, and on the way I do see Madeleine, and she sees me. She looks even better than ever, in this clingy low-cut dress, and I can see she obviously hasn't stopped swimming, and right away I'm thinking of the scene in the change room, on the towels, slipping inside her with stupid Duncan Young perving down. We have to pass each other to get to our places, and her smile drops, and she looks suddenly nervous. I get an urge to run for the toilet, the way my guts are churning over.

Hello Garvey, I heard you were presenting.

And you?

Now she looks curious instead of nervous.

Haven't you read your list? I'm up for best supporting actress. The one you're handing over.

I'm wondering if I could swap with another presenter, but these things are so highly organised, there's not much chance of that. As I'm wondering, Johnny Hearn swoops on Madelaine and takes her by the arm. C'mon, Maddy, they're waiting for us.

Mercifully I at least don't have to sit in the audience, like the other presenters, with everyone gawking at me and the cameras zooming in. Stuie's argued for me to be allowed to stay backstage, and only come out for the presentation, so I sit in a big chair and watch the awards on a monitor, when I can be bothered. The sound's right down, but it's not hard to tell what they're saying, thanks Mum, thanks Dad, thanks to the Almighty for giving me the strength to go on, I can't believe this is really happening, boo-hoo-hoo. Quite a few of them must be people I know, some I must even have worked with, but it's hard to recognise anybody, I've forgotten who's who in the business, and I suppose I don't really want to know anymore, somehow eating's all there is.

I've got a program, and from this I work out that Madeleine's up for her role in that low-budget feature she was doing just before *Fish out of Water* happened, when she played the girl having shock treatment. I'll bet she was good in it, too, though I haven't seen it, and probably won't, not now.

I'm wondering whether there's some food around, feeling desperately hungry, but then I'm being prodded to get out there. Another presenter announces me, and I walk out into the bright light, feeling like I've never been out in front of an audience before, wobbly on my feet. I get through those stupid jokes, though I can feel my timing's all wrong, and then, the envelope please, and then there it is, and the winner is … Madeleine Hill.

It all happens so fast, Madeleine's bouncing up the steps, bouncing boobs, nothing on under that dress, running towards me, arms around me, and kisses me like she's trying to show the world she still cares for me. Then words, lots of words, I'd like to thank, my mum, my dad, then names I don't quite register, my wonderful acting teacher, my wonderful co-stars, such a wonderful director to work for, my boyfriend Johnny who's taught me what it means to be an artist.

I've completely forgotten what I'm supposed to do next. All I can think of is wanting to grab her and kiss her and say, Madeleine, it's me, Garvey, remember, but she's out of there, right on cue, doesn't even look at me again. She has to run back down to the audience holding her award, while I get offstage as unobtrusively as possible, but I can't remember which way to go. Somebody's waving at me from the side, I think, but I wander over to the edge of the stage, those legs wobblier than ever, my bowels churning, and I can see Madeleine still running, and Johnny Hearn's standing, she's leaping into his arms, kissing and hugging, and somebody's calling me from behind, get off, and I turn to see, and then I'm floating backwards through the air, I feel so heavy, I land on something, I hit it like a ton of bricks, hearing broken glass, and screams. And then laughter, like it'll never end.

I wake up still in the Marlon Brando dinner suit, stinking from all the grog that was spilt on it when I landed on the table. I can dimly remember Stuie and the driver trying to get me out of the suit when they got me home, but they must have given up. I pull at it, it's so uncomfortable, but it won't come, and I get so angry I get up and look for something sharp. I find the breadknife, and slash the thing off me, down the sides of the legs, up each sleeve, Marlon Brando be buggered. The effort's got me sweaty, and just in my underdaks I wander out to see what there is left to eat. There's a king-sized pizza I didn't have time to eat last night when they came for me, which could be why I felt so wobbly. I hack it up into bits small enough to fit into the microwave, and pile them in, though I hate warmed-up stale pizza. While I'm waiting the door buzzer goes, and I ask who it is over the entryphone. It's Stuie, I've brought somebody to see you, he says, and I let them in. I don't bother covering up, everybody knows what I'm like anyway.

I wish I had put something on, though, because when Stuie steps inside he's got this woman with him. She's big and tall and broad shouldered, all muscley in a tight tracksuit, probably about forty-five but looking younger, though she's got this really hard hawky face under a crewcut, and a thick sinewy neck, and round her neck is a gold chain carrying what looks like a miniature Olympic gold medal. She's staring at me, with the most disgusted look I've ever seen, even more disgusted as she walks right round me to get the full picture. She pinches my belly and my bum, and feels up the tits I've developed where I used to have pecs.

Then she stands back and says, well, this is certainly a challenge to my professional abilities.

Excuse me?

Stuie steps in.

Meet Gerda Busch. Your personal trainer.

Oh, right.

I'd got so used to being like this I'd forgotten that somewhere along the line they were supposed to undo it all, help me get back to how I was. But that's almost too hard to imagine. Stuie butts in.

Roland Gussett helped you put it on, and now Gerda's going to help you take it off.

Gerda Busch looks over me again, even more sneery than before.

Roland Gussett doesn't know jack shit. I mean have you ever looked at the guy?

Just then the microwave bell goes off. Gerda Busch turns to it, hostile and suspicious.

What's that?

Oh, just a little snack I was warming up.

She opens the microwave door and pulls out the dish, piled so high with all the pieces of the king-sized pizza that barely fitted in, their cheese all melted in together.

Well, we do have a situation here, don't we?

Gerda Busch tosses the pizza into my garbage bin, and pulls a large Esky in from the hallway.

A journey of a thousand miles starts with a single step, she tells me, as she opens the Esky, and I'm looking down at containers full of things like bean sprouts, nuts, soy yoghurt, muesli and fruit salads. I'm already wondering if she's just going to leave this stuff and go, and I can get that pizza back out of the bin. But she's not going anywhere, and instead starts unrolling diet charts, a bit like the ones that Roland Gussett had, but these ones showing less and less food, not more and more. She stares at me again, as revolted as ever, and I wish I could cover up, I wish I could hide, I wish I could be brave enough to just say, sorry, forget the contract, you don't have to do anything for me, I'll just stay like I am, everything else is too hard to think about right now.

Before we start, I want to say one thing to you, Mr Quinn. You did this to yourself because you wanted to play that part to the best of your ability. Now you have to undo it because you want to get back to playing the part of the person you used to be. And if you don't want to play the part of Garvey Quinn, just as fiercely as you wanted to play Bryan Mars, there's not much I can do for you. I'm a professional, not a miracle worker.

The trouble is, I'm not sure how much I really did want to play Bryan Mars, I just kind of did it because everybody said it was a good idea. Now the same probably goes for going back to playing Garvey Quinn. I pick at the small breakfast she's allowed me, muesli and yoghurt and fruit salad, all the time wondering when KFC opens, and fearing what else she has in store for me. She stands over me watching, now and again flexing her big shoulders and arms, and I wonder if she might have been an Olympic discus thrower or some such, before she got into personal training. I'm waiting for her to get out a whip.

A mobile phone rings, which takes me by surprise, because the batteries ran out on mine weeks ago and I haven't bothered re-charging it since. And anyway, mine doesn't play 'The Bride of the Valkyries', out of *Apocalypse Now*, it's hers. She answers it, and says, come on up, I've left the door propped open. She must mean the security door at street level, because a minute later two large guys, body builders probably, carry in one of those big gym machines, with all the weights and pulleys and leg presses and arm presses and God knows what. Over there will do, she tells them, pointing to a corner of the room without bothering to consult me. They dump it down, then head out. They bring more loads, one of those ski machines where you pull on cables and your feet slide back and forth along the floor, and a treadmill with a big computer read-out that's supposed to tell me how fast I'm running and how many calories I'm burning up. They even bring in a couple of punching bags, a heavy bag and a speed bag, which the body builders attach to the doorjambs with a cordless drill they've brought along.

Stuie leaves when the body builders do, telling me I know you can do it, champ, and then I'm alone with the woman who's supposed to be going to change my life back to what it was. When I've finished my muesli, which seems like barely a mouthful, I'm put onto the treadmill. We'll start you off gently, she says, just a few minutes at first, while I work out exactly what I'm up against. Come on, get going.

Still just in my jocks, I try to work up a jog on the treadmill, but even making the wide strip of rubber move is an effort. I have to hold tightly onto the handle because I wobble so much, and I worry about tipping the whole thing over. I see the look on Gerda Busch's face get harder and harder, come on Mr Actor, you're doing ten minutes, come on, move your fat arse. I wish people would stop talking about my fat arse. I know it's fat, I thought that was the point.

I'm a wreck when she finally lets me stop, and I flop onto the sofa, drenched with sweat. No, come on, get up, you were an athlete before, try acting like one again. I'm made to do some stretching exercises, come on, there must still be some muscles in there somewhere, we don't want them stiffening up, do we? After the stretching I'm given some light gloves and put onto the speed bag, do this any time you feel like it, she tells me, imagine it's someone you hate and beat the crap out of them. A bit of aggression helps those calories burn faster, come on Mike Tyson, hit it!

I have no trouble imagining who I'm hitting, I grunt, this is for you, Seagrave, this is for you, Johnny Hearn, though I just can't get my hands to move fast enough to make the speed bag vibrate the way it's meant to, the way you see in old films of Muhammad Ali in training, just a blur. The bag just wobbles at the same speed as me. Then I'm made to lie down on the machine and do some sit-ups against a light weight, though at first I get my gut jammed between the bench and the handlebar, and she has to adjust it, which makes her look even more pissed off with me.

After about ten sit-ups I just lie there, I'm not doing anything more, no matter how rude she is. All right, that'll have to do, she says, I can see we're dealing with an attitude problem as much as a fat problem.

From the bench, I watch the next stage in her invasion of my flat. I can see through into the kitchen, where she's gone armed with a couple of big garbage bags. I see her crash around in the fridge, hurling everything in there into the bag, then go to the food cupboards and give them the same treatment. She dumps the garbage bags by the front door, then carries the Esky over to the fridge and starts unloading. Over here, big boy, she says. I wait to hear her say, move your fat arse, but this time she doesn't, and I go over to look. The plastic containers have labels, breakfast, lunch, dinner, snack, and they all look incredibly small.

This is your permitted calorie intake. Go over it and you're history, buster! I'll be here every morning for three hours, so don't think you can get away with any funny business.

When she's gone, I head straight for the lunch container, though it's really only morning tea time. It's got some slivers of smoked salmon, which are OK, though barely a mouthful, some cottage cheese, some sort of thin biscuits, and bits of celery and carrot. I eat it in about a minute, and then I start on dinner, which is some kind of pasta with a sauce on it that seems like it's made out of water it's so thin, and another fucking salad. I think about having tomorrow's breakfast as well, but if I'm having it in the morning when she arrives, I'm less likely to get caught out.

My big problem is that I haven't had to go food shopping for months, because while I was on the lardarse diet, it all got delivered. There's a takeaway just round the corner, and a mini-market, not that far away, but now that I look the way I do, and especially after the fuck-up at the AFI, I just can't find the courage. Plenty of guts but no courage, hah-hah.

By mid-afternoon though, my stomach's growling – the lack of food is almost painful, and I just can't put it off any longer. Moving as fast as I can, which isn't that fast, I try to keep close to buildings, in shadows, and I get to the takeaway without being spotted. I buy the last two roast chickens, a dozen pies, two dozen sausage rolls, and three of the biggest bucket of chips they've got. Then I go to the mini-mart, for a supersize tub of chocolate and tiramisu ice-cream, I get out cleanly, but halfway back towards home, I have to dodge two skateboarders whizzing down the footpath. They do U-turns as they pass me, coming back alongside, hey, it's Garvey Quinn, hey Garvey, what's for dinner? Suddenly people are swarming from everywhere, it's Garvey Quinn, look it's Garvey Quinn, I didn't know he was that fat!

I have to make the food last for the rest of the day, because there's no way I'm going out again. I have the last chip about mid-evening, then the bucket of ice-cream, and fall asleep quickly straight afterwards, probably exhausted from all that exercise. When I wake, the buzzer's going, it's Gerda Busch, but I realise I've left all the wrappers around the place, which stinks from all the takeaway. I tell her I'll be down in a minute, then open the windows wide, and bundle up all the rubbish. I'm about to throw it in the bin, but then I realise she'll probably have a look in there to check on me, so I shove it under the bed. When she comes in, with a strong wind flapping the curtains around, she stands in the middle of the room, sniffing.

Get a lot of food smells from the people across the hall, I tell her.

She looks in the fridge. You haven't had your breakfast, she says. You mustn't stop eating entirely, you know, we have to do this gradually.

The workout she puts me through this morning is far more intensive, the exercises still gentle ones, but lots of them, spread out over the whole three hours. As soon as she goes, I knock off today's lunch and dinner, plus the breakfast I should have had before, and tomorrow's as well, but it all slides straight down in a flash, and I know I have to do something drastic.

In the underground carpark I squeeze into my Subaru, wishing I had something roomier, like Bryan Mars's Landcruiser, as my gut pushes up against the steering wheel, even with the seat pushed right back. I keep a big floppy hat on, and sunglasses, and pull myself as low down in the car as I can, though that isn't easy – the only way I can get any lower is to spread, like a beanbag. I drive for nearly an hour, out to a shopping centre in a poor, mostly ethnic area, where I hope they're not too interested in which former soapie actor has turned into a hopeless joke. Hardly anybody looks at me, and when they do it's probably because I'm fat, not because I'm Garvey Quinn. I buy only as much as I can eat in one night. I don't dare keep any food in the flat for Gerda Busch to find, but I still end up with a whole trolley load by the time I'm done. I find some great Vietnamese duck, a good barbecue spare ribs place, and a stack of pastries full of vanilla cream from a Greek cake shop. There's a KFC as well, so I buy a couple of buckets, just to keep the intake up.

I get away with it, and then the next day, and the next

day, and the next. I know Gerda Busch is suspicious, but after each night's feast, I clean up everything, and at about two o'clock in the morning, take it out and dump it in a bin outside. Then in the morning I make sure I'm sitting having breakfast, just when Gerda Busch is due to arrive. I can tell she's still suspicious, especially after she puts me on the scales. In spite of stepping up the exercise, and the strict calorie control, I've gained a few more kilos.

Something is seriously wrong here, she says. Then she adds, the company's obligation to assist in your weight loss will cease the moment you are found to be consuming any other food than that prescribed in the program.

I know this, and probably I should care more, but even as she's talking to me, I'm thinking of big sticky pastries with dobs of cream. When I work out on the machines, the pastries are almost dancing in front of my eyes, they're about the only thing that's keeping me going, but I never catch them, and even though Gerda Busch stands there shouting at me, the treadmill seems to move slower than ever. When I switch to the ski machine I break a bearing on it, and it has to be taken away for repair.

Next morning when Gerda Busch arrives, one of her body builders is with her, holding the bin I dump my food wrappers in, with the KFC buckets sticking out the top.

This bin is allocated to flat number 2. That flat is currently unoccupied. How do you explain all this?

Don't know. Lots of people go by there, could have been anyone.

I know they're going to nail me, it's only a matter of time, but somehow getting food in this way gives my life some kind of meaning, a sense of purpose, you could call it, however feeble that might sound. Later that day I head off again, finding it even harder to squeeze myself into the Subaru, wondering if I should rent something bigger, but then I'd have to go somewhere, and show my driver's licence. Besides, I still like my little WRX, the way the turbo kicks in when you floor it, though it doesn't quite seem to have the get up and go it used to, especially up hills.

I buy up big, really big, lots of those Vietnamese ducks, masses of chips and potato wedges, some thick, cheesy lasagne, and some moussaka for a bit of variety. I pop all this in the front seat, along with the KFC, my mouth watering on the drive home, my stomach growling in anticipation. For the last stretch of my trip back to the flat, I always detour into some back streets, a bit further to go, but it keeps me off the main drag. That's packed full of flash cafes, places where media people and models and the rest of them hang out, good fun to live near in the old days, especially with Madeleine, but pretty dangerous territory now. But two blocks from home, taking the last corner before the alleyway that gets me to the back of the building, there's a roadblock, those black and orange barriers and guys fixing a water main or something. I've got no choice but to go right round, past the cafes, until I get to the other end of the alleyway. I figure I'll probably be all right, they're probably all too caught up in themselves to notice a guy in a Subaru with a hat on, and I'm almost level with the last of them, but then this drunk wanders across and I have to brake hard not to hit him, and the car behind me rams the Subaru right up the bum.

It doesn't feel like I'm injured, but I can see people coming from all over the place, and my first thought is just to run as best I can, forget the car, grab the ducks and just try to disappear into the dark. When I try to get out of the car, though, I find I can't, the shove in the back has rammed my gut right up under the steering wheel, I wasn't wearing my seatbelt because it won't adjust far enough anymore. I know there are faces looking in at me, but I try not to look back. Somebody must know me, because a voice calls out, Garvey, are you all right?, and then the cries start to go up, it's Garvey Quinn, it's Garvey Quinn!

The police are on the scene pretty quickly, moving the people back a few feet. One of them looks in the window at me, like he thinks it's funny, looks like a dynamite job, he says. In fact they call for the rescue squad; they're going to use some sort of machine to cut the whole car away around me, but it's a long time coming, probably because the ambulance man's had a poke at me and told them I'm not urgent. So the people just keep standing, looking, some of them have gone back and got their cappuccinos or their drinks, and one's munching on a brioche that squishes out vanilla cream every time he bites into it, which makes me even hungrier. The food's all there beside me, I've been trying not to think about it, but I notice that the crash has popped the top off the KFC bucket, and there are some chicken nuggets lying on the seat, and I reach over for one, I can just get it into my mouth in one quick pop, without being too obvious. That's when the first flash goes off, and as I turn to see what it is it goes off again, so I'm looking right into the camera, the chicken nugget held high.

There's nothing wrong with me, but they keep me in hospital overnight anyway. A young Chinese doctor, leaning over to examine the bruise that the steering wheel's left on my gut, gives it a poke, just like everybody else seems to want to do. He asks me, is there a history of obesity in your family?

Not until now, I say. I lie there wondering what's become of the food, those Vietnamese ducks especially, probably a big blow-out for the tow truck driver and his mates back at the base. When I get out in the morning and hail a taxi, I'm lucky to be a dazed-looking nightshift driver's last passenger, and he doesn't seem to notice who or what I am. I get him to put me out a block from the flat, at the mini-market, where I pick up some frozen pizzas and instant chips, not what I'd like, but it will have to do. As I shuffle up to my building, there's Gerda Busch, standing with her body builder henchmen. I wonder if she's going to get them to beat the crap out of me for disobedience, but she could do it herself just as easily. I don't need to look to know what's in the morning paper she's holding, but she forces me to as I come closer, virtually shoving it in my face.

Startled by the flash, I've got my eyes wide open, and my mouth open too, and my hand is just lowering the chicken nugget into it. The headline says, Hunky soap star turns to roles of fat.

Yes I know, I say, not bothering to try to hide my new stash of food.

Due to this breach of your obligations, you are entitled to no further assistance from us.

OK, I say.

In fact the body builders are there to take away the exercise equipment, which is fine by me. When they're gone, I thaw out the frozen food, which tastes like cardboard, but at least it's something to put in my mouth. Just as I'm lying back after I've eaten it, wondering how to get more food now that I don't have a car, the buzzer rings. I try to ignore it, I don't want to see anyone ever again. But whoever it is just goes on and on, and finally I get up and go to the window. Down below I see Dad, and my brother Dean, who's got his work truck, the F100, with Dean Quinn, Licensed Plumber and Gasfitter written on the side. When I press the entryphone I hear Dad's growly voice.

Let us in son. We've come to take you home.

GarVEY QUiNN

Then I hear Dean's voice, scratchy because he's too far from the entryphone.

Yeah you dickhead. What have you done to yourself?

★ ★ ★

BRYAN MARS

You've been ignoring them for weeks and weeks now – you even pulled the phone right out of the wall, you were so annoyed about it ringing at all hours. You don't read the notes under the door, either, and there are so many there now they've jammed up the gap. You're not even exactly sure any longer how much time has gone by since they found you and locked you away in here, put you on ice, but it must be quite a while. What you don't know, either, is how long it takes to make a movie, but they must have been working on it for ages. If you were still reading all those magazines that Mum used to bring in, still watching all those TV junk shows, you'd probably know exactly what was up, but you felt better keeping yourself in the dark.

You know, though, that something must be going to change for you before too long, because they wouldn't be going to just pay to keep you here indefinitely, no matter how much money they've got to chuck around. They've got a plan, and you're in it, and you wish you know what it is. But somehow you know you're not going to let them get away with it, not that Seagrave filth. That's what you think of as you pound up and down, back and forth along the balcony, round through the rooms and out again. They've made a movie with you looking like a blimp when they said they wouldn't, they've paid heaps to keep you out of the limelight, and given you everything they thought you wanted, so what's their payoff?

You're wondering exactly that when you hear banging on the door, which you knew would happen sooner or later. You could ignore that too, let them bang till their hand hurts, but then you hear a voice call out. We know you're in there Mars, and you've got to listen. And you do listen, because you know that finally you're ready.

Yeah, what do you want?

Be ready tomorrow. We're flying you back to Sydney.

What if I don't want to go?

You have to go. Don't you remember the terms of your contract?

No.

Which is true. At that stage you were letting your mum do all the decision-making, you just wanted everything to go away.

You have to go. *Fish Out of Water* opens next week.

What's that got to do with me?

Mr Mars, you're aware that if you refuse to co-operate, we can no longer offer you the legal protection you've so far enjoyed.

Which gets you thinking even more. If they take away their crash-hot lawyers and encourage people to make trouble for you over the fake suicide, what's the worst that can happen to you? You'll get put in gaol, but that's more or less where you've been for the last few years anyway. You don't say anything, let them do the worrying.

In case you're anxious about having to travel on an airliner, Mr Mars, that's all taken care of. Mr Seagrave has hired a private plane and he'll be coming here personally to accompany you back. That's an indication of the high regard in which he holds you. Please be ready.

You're ready, for whatever, but you bet Seagrave's not. You pick at a bit of the food that keeps on coming, just skim a bit off the top as you go by, and leave the rest to rot. You don't pack or anything, just stay as you are, you've done the best you can with those floppy clothes, they'll just have to accept what they get. By the afternoon you're excited, you can hardly wait anymore, and when at last you hear the knock, you run straight over and throw open the door, wanting to see his face.

Seagrave just stands there looking at you, his jaw hanging down.

How nice to see you, Mr Seagrave.

Then you hear the words start to come out. You arsehole, you fucking fucking fucking piece of shit. Fuck fuck fuck fuck fuck, you fucking fucking cunt. How could you fucking do this to me?

You watch him, wondering what he's going to do next. He steps back a bit, turns around, scratches his face, turns back at you, like he can't quite figure where he is, or what's happening. Then you watch him sort of focus, look at you again, this time without the swearing. You hear him say again, how could you do this to me?

You pretend not to notice. You just tell him, ready to go when you are.

You see him back off, looking like he just wants to run and hide.

Look, thanks anyway, Bryan, you hear him say. But just thinking this through, why don't you just stay on here a bit longer? You've probably suffered enough already, so why don't you just go on staying out of the limelight? I'll get them to pay another year's rent on this place, and we'll just keep everything as it was, all right?

StUffED

You watch him running away. You didn't think you were going to get on that plane, but you're not staying here anymore, why should you?

*　*　*

GarVEY QUiNN

Dad reckons I'm a disgrace to the family. He says there's nothing wrong with a bit of a beergut, lots of blokes have them, he's got a bit of a one himself. But letting the blubber build up all over every part of you so it just hangs off in rolls that keep on wobbling even after you've stopped moving, in Dad's eyes that's a sure sign of someone who doesn't know how to control himself, someone who's thick as two short planks and weak as piss. I agree, but that doesn't make me want my food any less.

On the other hand, Dad doesn't try to make me do anything about it, other than keeping out of view. He says a man's fate is in his own hands, which shows how little he knows about the world, even at his age. When he and Dean came over and brought me back in the truck, the first thing he did was get out Dean's old barbell and dumbells, which Dean hadn't had much use for since things happened with Jodie. Dad just plonked them in the middle of the floor, didn't say a word. Though since then, every now and then, like just in passing he'll say, those heavy enough for you, we can whack some more weights on them anytime you like, and I'll say, thanks Dad. He also put an exercise bike in my bedroom, one that one of the neighbours was throwing out, but I think it would probably break if I got on it. I know he meant well, but if Gerda Busch couldn't get things happening, Dad doesn't have a prayer.

When it came to food, at first he tried to pretend things were just like they were when I last lived at home, which is a few years ago now. So breakfast would be cornflakes, two eggs, bacon, and a couple of pieces of toast and vegemite. To some people that probably sounds a lot, but for me it hardly touched the sides. Dinner was a steak about the size of a man's hand, or a couple of chops, a couple of potatoes, two veg, some tinned pineapple or peaches for dessert, and maybe a scoop or two of ice-cream. Lunch would be sandwiches, and if Dad was going to be out, he'd say, there's some bread and ham, or cheese or whatever, you can make yourself a sandwich if you get hungry. And I'd look in the fridge as soon as he got out the door, and there'd be a packet of bread with about three slices left in it, and a couple of bits of that ready-sliced ham, going grey at the edges because the packet had been left open.

So it wasn't long after I first moved back that I knew I had to do something. Without a car, I had Buckley's of getting away with anything, but one night, in the second week, after I'd used up every old rust-spotted tin of Spam and baked beans and the like from down the back of the food cupboard, some of them with use by dates you wouldn't want to think about, I chose my moment. Dad was asleep, sprawled out in front of the TV, bored shitless by a tennis match, and I just stepped outside and started walking. I'm not sure I would have taken Dad's car even if he hadn't been sleeping with the keys in his pocket, and I knew I was in for a hard night, but you'll do anything when you're desperate. Our place is miles from any shops, it's not like in the city where you can just step outside and find whatever you want a block away. Out here, to get anything, you have to drive, and if you can't, you're cactus.

GARVEY QUINN

Even though the first few blocks took forever, at least they were in the dark, so though people in passing cars could spot my bulk, they couldn't make out my face. All I got were a few U-ies and wheelies next to me and shitheads calling out, it's the blob, it's the blob! or, you're so fat! That I could live with, but then the lighting got brighter, and the first thing I had to pass was a service station, and right away someone serving himself at a pump called out, Hey, you're Garvey Quinn. So pretty soon I had the whole thing again, the crowd following, some on foot, some of them crawling along in their cars, it's Garvey Quinn, it's Garvey Quinn. But I pushed on, the couple more blocks to the takeaway, bought some barbecue chooks and half a dozen each of Chiko rolls and battered savs. On the trip back the mob was even bigger, and I wanted to run, but I knew I'd look even more ridiculous. I thought of just sitting down on the road, hoeing into the food and just not getting up again until they all finally went away. But you can't do that sort of thing, not in real life, so I just kept walking, and each block felt longer and longer.

Then a car pulled up really close, too close, like somebody was going to do something to me, and I speeded up my shuffle just a bit. That was when I heard Dad's voice, get in, son. While I worked my way into the car, Dad got out and faced the mob, and he shouted, all right you lot, piss off or I'll do the lot of you, don't think I fucking won't! Then we drove home, and all Dad said on the way was, luckily my mate at the servo spotted you, told me you were out making a spectacle of yourself. Jesus was he right.

Next morning though, Dad said to me, time we got this place better stocked with food. You want to make a shopping list, I'll bring some stuff home tonight.

I made a great shopping list, so many legs of lamb and beef and ham and dozens of eggs and buckets of ice-cream, and every kind of cheese, we had to connect the old spare fridge that's been in the garage for years. Next list I got a bit fancier, duck, and some fancy sauces, so I could try to learn to do that nice Vietnamese duck like that bastard tow truck driver must have scored the night of the accident. I gave Dad one of my ATM cards and told him my PIN, and he just kept on coming back with food and pretending none of it was happening, something he's pretty good at, just kept on cooking his own steak and two veg. I at least had something to do with myself again, cooking more or less all day, experimenting, eating, cooking, eating some more, and it more or less kept my mind from coming too close to what had got me into the situation in the first place. At least for a time, until Stuie knocked on the door.

If you don't show, you realise you'll never work again, Stuie says.

I don't want to work again. I mean, who'd hire me?

It's a lot more than your job prospects we're talking about. You are contracted to get out there and promote the film. I've been keeping them at bay for weeks, saying you were sick, but the fucking thing opens next week, and if you don't get out there, they'll go for the jugular. They'll sue you for everything you've got. Do you want to end up with nothing?

How much more harm can anybody do to me?

Yeah? Well before you get too self-pitying, ask yourself how you're going to pay your food bills once they clean you out.

Once he says that, I realise I've got no choice. Pride's one thing but food's another. The following morning a stretch limo turns up outside, before Dad's left for work. I hadn't told him anything, I couldn't bring myself to, and he looks like he could kill me.

GarVEY QUiNN

What the fuck's that thing doing in my driveway?

Sorry Dad. Got a bit of work to do. Can't get out of it.

I try not to look at him as I lever myself into the big double width rear compartment, but I know he's standing on the front step with his arms folded, and he calls out just as the driver's closing the door after me.

If only you'd taken that bloody plumber's apprenticeship!

With me in the back of the limo is one of those blonde publicity ladies in a short black skirt, the sort who buzz around when something's been released. I can never think of anything to say to them, I always have a feeling they wouldn't understand. She's trying to pretend she's got heaps of room, but really she's squeezed up against the door.

Haven't you done this sort of thing before, she asks me? I thought you would have known to dress a bit better.

This is the only thing I've got that fits, I tell her.

I'm wearing my new supersize shirt, about the size of a car cover for a VW beetle, and trousers with legs that look like those canvas camping toilets you hang from a tree branch. Dad took my measurements with one of his work tapemeasures and got Auntie Janice to make me an outfit. She's pretty big herself, so she was only too glad to help.

If that's really all you've got, you're going to have to act very casual, she tells me. Very jolly. Make it very clear you're comfortable with what you've done for the sake of this great movie. A joke or two would help, maybe something like, sorry, I had to wear this, Marlon Brando's suit didn't arrive in time.

Jolly and casual are about the last thing I feel. At the TV station I start dripping with sweat, before I've even got out under the lights. The make-up girls are slapping more and more stuff onto me to stop me shining, but there's nothing they can do, I just keep dripping through it, and they talk to each other about me, things like, shit, what are we going to do with him, this is disgusting. My clothes are drenched too, huge sweaty circles spreading out from my armpits and glueing the cloth to my flesh. Somebody goes off to do a frantic search through wardrobe for some old costume that might fit, but the only thing anywhere near my size is an elephant suit from a kids' show. Someone suggests taking out all the padding and cutting the head off and seeing how it looks on me, but in the end I go on as I am, the two circles of armpit sweat now meeting in the middle. I hear the chat show host, Tamsin Youl, give her introduction, and I know what I'm in for.

Ladies and gentlemen, if you've ever wondered just how far some actors are prepared to go to play a part, our next guest will be an eye-opener. In fact you'll need your eyes pretty wide open to be able to see all of him at once. Once the svelte young Doctor Simon Dennis in *Medical Emergency*, Garvey Quinn has just finished playing the biggest role of his life, and I do mean big! Before his new movie *Fish Out of Water* has even been released, there are already industry rumours that Garvey has been signed up for the latest remake of *Moby Dick*, and guess which part Garvey will be playing. Ladies and gentlemen, please welcome, the hu-u-u-uge Garvey Quinn!

There's a fanfare of excited music from the studio band, and a burst of applause, but almost as soon as I step out into the lights, everything goes silent. Even the band cuts out, the trombone fizzling out with a funny farting downward note like they do in cartoon soundtracks. There are gasps of disbelief and even some groans as I waddle over to where Tamsin Youl is standing next to the two armchairs and coffee table that make up the set. I haven't met her before, I was so long in make-up we didn't get to have a preliminary chat, but I've been told we're supposed to kiss when I go over. Trying hard to hold it all together and do what's wanted, I lean over to try to peck her cheek, but she pulls back. She looks like she's trying to keep it all together too.

Well, Garvey, there's certainly a lot of you, isn't there?

I figure I'd better try a joke, right now. The joke.

Yes. Sorry I came dressed like this. Marlon Brando's suit didn't arrive in time.

On some other occasion the audience controller's frantic signalling just might have squeezed a laugh out of the crowd for that, but this time it gets what it deserves. In the deathly silence, Tamsin Youl gestures towards an armchair.

Well, Garvey, why don't you take the weight off your feet.

She's looking at her autocue and I see on it that she's to start by asking how difficult it's been transforming myself like this.

Seriously Garvey, this has been quite a transformation, hasn't it? I mean, to play the part of Bryan Mars as he apparently is now, you've had to make yourself truly enormous. How difficult has that been?

It's only now, trying to come up with an answer, that I realise how little there is in my head except what I'm going to eat next. I'd almost forgotten that I made myself like this for a reason, I can hardly even remember that I'm an actor, I'm just someone who eats.

Um, it wasn't that hard, really.

As soon as I've said it, I know from the little twitch of Tamsin Youl's upper lip that they expect much better from a professional like me, and I wish I could deliver. Tamsin Youl pushes on.

But it must have taken real discipline. Special diets, a whole new structure to your life.

No, I just ate a lot.

StUffED

I know that answer's pathetic too, but just saying it makes me remember the first really big blow-out meal I had in my caravan on the set, when Roland Gussett's cook did a Texan chicken fried steak, and I can't stop myself licking my lips.

Then I see from the autocue Tamsin Youl's about to get onto my well-known public stuff-ups. Her face goes all serious.

It hasn't been easy for you, though, has it? I mean we've all seen the newspaper stories, the humiliating photographs, and none of us will easily forget the disaster of the AFI awards. What sort of a toll has this taken on your private life?

Er, quite a big one.

The stories are that you keep a pretty low profile these days, and looking at you it's not hard to understand why. Do you think there'll be a time when your life returns to normal?

Don't know, I say. As I answer, I'm singeing the steak just slightly before I plunge it into an inch-deep pool of chicken fat and turn the heat up under the pan.

I hear her sigh. I see from the autocue she's got to get onto the film itself, and its subject.

Now, the real person you're playing in *Fish Out of Water*, Bryan Mars, is something of a tragic figure, isn't he? Here was someone we all admired greatly, a gorgeous young hero who seemed to have the world at his feet, and yet who somewhere went terribly wrong. What sort of responsibility do you feel towards him, in a sense taking over his life like this? Did you ever feel uneasy about it?

I don't know.

This answer isn't because I'm thinking about food, but because she's started hitting me with words like responsibility. Now she's winding it up, obeying signals from the producer to get me off fast.

One last question, Garvey, as we can see, you did a great job of putting the weight on for this role. How are you going with the job of getting it off?

Not so great.

Well, I'm sure we'll all be wishing you the best of luck. Ladies and gentlemen, a big round of applause for Garvey Quinn!

Dad watches the show when it goes to air that night, though I don't want him to, but he turns it off halfway through, when she asks whether there'll ever be a time when my life returns to normal and I say I don't know.

Why the fuck did you let them do it to you? he shouts at me.

It's not that I haven't been asking that question myself, but all I can think of is that with all my energy taken up with eating, I didn't have the strength left to resist, and maybe I really wanted it to be a debacle anyway, just to get me out of this sooner rather than later. But I just tell Dad the obvious.

They told me if I didn't go on the show, they'd do me like a dinner.

Dad just shakes his head and walks away. It occurs to me how much I relate things to food and eating these days. I could just as easily have answered him, if I didn't, they would have had me for breakfast. They'd have made mincemeat out of me. They'd have had me on toast.

Then the publicity lady rings. She tells me her phone has been running hot with all the people who had been going to interview me saying they want to cancel, and she says she doesn't blame them one bit, that was the most pathetic interview she's ever seen. I'm not too worried about that, and hope that as I at least made myself available, nobody's going to try suing me. I decide to have a serious go at cooking that Vietnamese duck.

★ ★ ★

BRYAN MARS

The last thing you do before you leave is shave off the beard you always hoped would stop people recognising you, but never did. Then you walk out with your bag, you take the lift down, but you get out at the ground floor, not the basement which was how you came in, and you walk straight out into the street. There are people all around, it's mid-morning, busy, and you walk amongst them, the way you'd thought about when all you could do was look down from the balcony. You wait for someone to recognise you, for just one moment you think, what if you've got this all wrong, what if they don't want you back. You know it's too late now, though, you've set this thing in motion.

It's not until you're in the barber shop, two blocks away, that it happens. You lower yourself into the chair, and as the barber ties the white sheet onto you, you see his eyes give a bit of a blink. He steps back and says to you, smiling, I just figured out who you are. You're Bryan Mars.

That's right.

You see his hand come out to meet yours, and you take it, and you hear him say, it's a real honour to meet you. He stands back to look at you again and says, there were stories about you being as big as an elephant, just goes to show you, don't believe what you hear, eh?

Too right, you tell him.

StUffED

I've seen jockeys who are fatter than you are. Hey, you lot, come out and see who's in the chair.

The other barber comes out from the back room, and the apprentice, and they shake your hand too, they say what an honour it is, and the apprentice asks, do you think that world record of yours will ever be broken?

Bound to happen one of these days, you say.

Then the barber says, I remember how you used to have your hair, lots of guys used to come and ask me to cut their hair just like yours.

He does a good job on you, too, re-shaping your wild haystack of hair, and then your next stop is at a clothes shop for something that fits properly. You want just one outfit for now, you'll worry about getting something more formal once you get down south. As you're coming out of the fitting room, you're recognised again, must be even easier now with the hair right, and you're told, I don't believe that was you at all, a while back when they sprung some gutso on the TV, why don't those bastards try giving us the truth for a change.

You go to a cafe and have a light lunch, just some fish and a salad, and you keep getting, hey, aren't you Bryan Mars? and you keep saying, yes I am, and you feel all right. Then the cafe owner comes over with a magazine, he's got it open at a picture of you leaping off the blocks at what looks like the Commonwealth Games, it's a story about the movie coming out.

Mr Mars, would you mind signing this for me? I'll get it framed and put it up on the wall there, pride of place.

You sign best wishes, Bryan Mars.

I keep reading stuff about this movie they've made about you. Have you heard about it?

Yeah, a bit.

Doesn't sound like much chop. Jesus, look at this.

You're shown another page where that actor, Garvey Quinn, is sitting in what looks a like a TV studio, on the set of some chat show. He's enormous, as enormous as you were at the worst of it, and he's soaked with sweat, looking scared and uncomfortable and just plain stupid.

I saw that show when he was on it. Was the most pathetic thing I've ever seen. I mean, look at the guy, look what he's done to himself. They were going on about how he went to all the trouble of doing that so he could play you as you really are, but Jesus, you're not like that. You're nothing like that.

No.

Doesn't say much for their accuracy, does it. Makes you wonder what the rest of the movie's going to be like. And as for that Garvey Quinn, he could hardly string two words together, it was like there was nobody home, it doesn't make you want to fork out money to see him act. When I fork out money, I expect to see a real hero, like you.

As you leave he adds, it's a crying shame the way they set out to destroy somebody special, but let me tell you, I never believed any of their lies, and there's plenty of other people feel the same way as I do.

Everywhere you go it's much the same. You even think of trying to head down south by bus, or even hitch-hiking, so you can show up at lots of places, you're enjoying it so much. There isn't time, though, not this time, so you get the most you can out of what's possible, the bus ride out to the airport, the hanging around in the departure lounge, the flight itself. All the way it's, excuse me, aren't you Bryan Mars? and such a pleasure to meet you, and once a champion always a champion. People reach for any bit of paper they can find, and you gladly sign best wishes from Bryan Mars, and your signature flows onto the paper the way it always did, never the slightest variation, which is what people like, so it's obvious it was really you.

On the plane they move you up to business class so you can have a bit more peace, what with all the wellwishers, not that you mind. Part of the way into the flight, the captain invites you up into the cockpit to have a bit of a yarn. The hostess, conveying the message, tells you he doesn't usually do this, he's a bit fussy about who he lets in.

In the front, you've got a great view of the desert passing underneath you. The pilot says to be honest, when they told me Bryan Mars was going to be on my plane, my first thought was, will we have enough engine power to get off the ground? Will he wreck the plane? After what I'd heard about you. Then I had a little peek back into the cabin and saw you. It makes you wonder whether you can ever believe anything anymore. I mean, I remember way back, when all those pictures started to appear, of you getting in trouble in nightclubs and all of that. I remember thinking, what a pathetic excuse for a human being. Now I'd say, there must have been more to it than what we could see. I can tell that by meeting you. You can't fake dignity.

You tell him, thank you. Thank you very much. It seems that all anybody wants is for you to feel good, and you do, you feel great. That is until you step out into the airport at the other end and see the newspaper banner and rush over and read the front page story there in the shop. You say please, no, don't let it end like that. They don't deserve to get out of it that easily.

* * *

GarVEY QUiNN

A voice says to me, Looks like it could be your lucky day.

All this eating makes me sleep well. Despite all my worries, every night I'm out to it, ten hours straight, like a big fat corpse. So when I first hear Dad talking to me, standing over the bed, I can't make out who he is or what the hell he's on about.

What?

Seems that filth of a director might have cooked his own goose.

Goose, I think. Cooked. Yeah, I'd like that. Coming out of the oven crisp and brown on a big steel baking dish, in a big pool of its juice.

Goose, I say to the person, who I've now worked out is Dad. I look up to see him brandishing the morning newspaper.

Wake up you boofhead, he says. Something's come up that might be going to save your bacon.

Bacon? I say. This seems to make Dad annoyed, for some reason.

For Christ's sake stop thinking about food for a minute and listen to me, he says. There's been a big development. Look.

I prop myself up and have a look at the paper. The

headline says, Swim pic in hot water, and there's a photo of me and Seagrave on the set, an early pool scene with me looking super fit, my Speedos wet and clinging to me. There's also a smaller photo of two people I don't know, a man and a woman, though she looks a bit familiar. I snatch the paper out of Dad's hands and start reading.

For the first time in months I feel a moment of real satisfaction, triumph even, as I see proof that smart bastard genius Stirling Seagrave doesn't know everything after all. The woman in the smaller picture is Vicki Michaels, the real one, and the man is her husband, Gunnar Lofgren, the mighty Swedish pole vaulter who snatched her away from poor tubby, waddling Bryan. Since then Gunnar, as much a hero in his own country as Bryan ever was here, has made it into parliament, and Vicki's studied law and is now lecturing at the University of Malmo. The two of them have been shown a script of *Fish out of Water*, and they're ropeable, and why wouldn't they be? They say the movie portrays Vicki as a sex-mad bimbo without a trace of dignity or intelligence. They also say it's unfair in its portrayal of her as heartlessly walking out on Bryan in his darkest hour when, according to her, their split was by mutual agreement. They've hired top legal representation here, and the producers have been hit with an injunction, just days before the premiere. What Gunnar and Vicki want is for all copies of the movie to be destroyed, but for a start they want the premiere called off.

I can't say I'm surprised. A number of times I thought, how can they get away with this? I figured they were all right with Bryan, they had him all tied up legally so he couldn't interfere, but there were other people involved. On the other hand, Seagrave wasn't the only person in the company – there must have been others around the place who knew what they were doing, so I never opened my mouth. Fat lot of good it would have done if I had.

That make you feel a bit happier, son? Dad asks me.

Yeah, a bit, I say.

Jesus I hope they win, Dad goes on. Wipe out every last trace of that movie and then you can forget it ever happened, get all that disgusting weight off your carcass and go out and get a proper job like I bloody told you to in the first place, next time when your dad gives you some advice maybe you'll fucking listen.

Dad stamps out after that, he's never been someone who stays happy for long, and as soon as I've downed a half dozen fried eggs and a plateful of toast, I get on the phone to Stuie. I've still got the last slice of toast in my mouth when he answers, and my words must be a bit garbled from the chewing. I say, hello Stuie, it's Garvey here, and he snaps back right away, do you have to talk to me with your mouth full? Sorry, I mumble, and gulp down the rest. Then I ask him, do you know what's going on with the movie?

Not much, Stuie answers. I spent all day yesterday trying to get through to Seagrave's office once I heard something was up. Finally at about six o'clock I got through to some script girl or something, sounded like she was in tears, Seagrave must have put a rocket up her. When I told her who I was and said if she wanted to get on in the industry she'd need an agent, she told me what she knew, which, as I said, wasn't much. I've got to tell you, I didn't have Stephen Hawking on the other end of the phone.

I'm not familiar with every name in the film industry and I tell him, just get to the point, Stuie.

It seems they're re-cutting like mad. Seagrave's determined to go through with the premiere, even if it kills everyone in the company except him. And they're applying to have the injunction lifted, on the grounds that this is a story of national importance, it's part of the country's mythology, and why should a couple of foreigners tell the Australian public what they can and can't see? Vicki's a Swedish citizen now, you see. Then Stuie adds, and I've got to say, I agree completely, what's it got to do with them?

I ask him, whose side are you on? And it looks like this is one of those days when everything I say just seems to make people angry. Stuie shouts back down the phone at me.

Get a grip on yourself, Garvey. Just remember, if they succeed in killing this movie, your career dies too.

It's dead anyway, I tell him. That just gets him going even more.

Don't talk crap. You'll be up on the screen, an actor doing a job. You were asked to play fat, and you played fat. If you did it well you succeeded. So did you do it well?

Yeah, I suppose, only …

Only nothing! Your career will be determined by the judgements of professionals who want to know whether you can act, not by sniggering morons who think it's funny when you get stuck in a doorway.

I tell him Stuie, you know this business is mostly about what you look like. He pauses before he answers me.

Well, for a fat man, you look pretty good.

Barely a minute after I've finished talking to Stuie, the phone rings. By that stage I'm back in the kitchen studying the contents of the fridge, contemplating an early lunch, maybe something a bit special to get me through what looks like being a very worrying time. I'm not sure what I hope will happen, either, because on the one hand, if the movie is killed off, I'll have done this to myself for absolutely nothing. On the other hand, if it goes ahead, a whole lot more people will get to see how stupid I look. So I let the phone just ring and ring while I search for the kilo of king prawns

GARVEY QUINN

I asked Dad to get, and finally the ringing stops.

I find the prawns tucked away behind a big bag of ham hocks which I asked for more out of curiosity than anything, I've always wondered what you do with them. I decide to have the prawns by themselves, lightly fried in garlic, as an entrée to something more substantial, maybe a whole chook if I can get it into the oven in time, though then again the leg of lamb looks nice, with a few sprigs of rosemary. I go for the lamb, I hold it up to admire the nice marbling in the meat, and then the phone rings again. I let it ring a few times, but finally I decide I better see who it is, just in case it's Stuie with more news. I used to say 'This is Garvey' when I answered the phone, but now I just say, 'Hello'.

Garvey, mate, how you going, I hear, but I've got no idea who it is. Who is this?

Len Buckler, I interviewed you for *TV Soaps* a couple of years back. I'm with the *Tele* now, you're probably familiar with my showbiz column.

Er, no. Actually I think I can just picture him, big-eared freckly guy who laughed at everything I said about what it was like being in *Medical Emergency*, as if he'd never heard anyone quite so stupid. But then he wrote the standard feel-good piece, young actor with a bright future, quoting me saying stuff like, we're all deeply committed to the show, I believe that people identify with my character because of his integrity and sense of purpose, it's a great cast to work with, we're one big happy family, of course I'd love to do a movie one day if a decent role came along, blah blah blah. Reading it you'd never have guessed he thought I was a complete shithead. I ask him, what can I do for you? and I take another look at the lamb leg before I put it down, thinking what a great lunch it'll be if I can just get this guy off the phone.

Can you tell me how you feel about all this, Garvey?

StUffED

The way this legal shit's hitting the fan?

Oh, is it?

Don't pretend you don't know, mate. You're the star of the show, your arse is on the line as much as anyone's, maybe even more because there's so much of it.

I wonder if this is some journalist's technique, insult people to get them talking. I tell him, I've got nothing to say.

He comes back, if it was me I'd be spitting chips, how are you going to feel if the producers have turned you into a human haystack and it's all for nothing?

Luckily I remember a line I heard some other actor say in an interview once. I tell him, I have absolute faith in the producers' integrity.

There's this snorting laughter coming out of the phone. Do you? Buckler asks me. So it's not true what everyone's saying, that Seagrave's a raving loony and the movie's a farcical cesspit?

Goodbye Mr Buckler, I'm going to hang up now.

Wait wait wait, he shouts at me down the phone. Don't you think you owe it to yourself to tell your side of the story? Just listen to me, I'm offering you one last chance. To come out of this with at least a molecule of self-respect. And maybe the public's respect as well. What I'm suggesting is this. You tell your story to me. Exclusively. About what it was like to be exploited by Seagrave. Talk about the plight of an innocent young actor tricked into blowing-out his once beautiful body into a disgusting pile of blubber because everybody said this was going to be great art. The public hates art, so you'll have them eating out of your hand.

I ask him, but what if they don't manage to kill the movie? And what if it's a success?

Well then, he says, then you'll be Mr Controversial, public

acclaim isn't what matters to you, you don't take shit from anyone. Think Sean Penn. Think Russell Crowe. Think, um, Oliver Reed.

That just isn't me, I tell him.

It will be, he says. We'll photograph you looking sad and thoughtful, maybe in your lounge room, sitting back in the sofa, not a morsel of food in sight, unshaven, maybe still in your pyjamas.

I don't wear pyjamas. They don't fit anymore.

And up on the wall behind you, there'll be a big framed portrait of you in *Medical Emergency*, the full deal, white coat, stethoscope, cheekbones.

I don't want this. Apart from anything else, if I let a photographer into the house, Dad would kill me, and probably stop doing the shopping as well.

Of course, if you don't want to co-operate, that's fine too, says Buckler. You'll be in the news anyway, and we'll just run the file picture of you jammed in your car with the chicken nugget heading straight for your gob. Thought you might be sick of seeing that by now.

That's when I hang up. What stops me in the end is just one thought: What would Madeleine say when she found out I'd rejected art? I know the answer, of course, she'd say, he was just a soapie hack all along, he wasn't prepared to sacrifice his pretty boy ego in the interests of really becoming the character. I feel it would be her I'd be betraying, whether she could care anymore or not.

Len Buckler was lying when he said if I didn't co-operate they'd just keep reusing the shot of me jammed in the WRX. After I've polished off the prawns and the leg of lamb, I take the garbage round to the wheelie bin at the side of the house. My cooking produces so much rubbish it's not fair to leave it all to Dad, even though he's ordered me to stay indoors, and anyway the bins are well sheltered behind a wall of lattice. So I'm surprised when I hear the click of a camera just as I'm cramming the garbage bag into the top of the wheelie bin, sweating and groaning. Worse, I'm wearing nothing but an old length of curtain wrapped round me like a sarong, and there's plenty of rippling flab on display. There's nothing I can do, and I just wait until the motor drive stops clicking. If I don't turn round at least they won't see I've got half a muffin in my mouth.

It's that photograph they use a day later when the news comes through that Seagrave's succeeded in having the injunction lifted, and the premiere is going ahead. The headline over the photo of me and the bin reads, He's a wheelie big star!, and just to rub it in the caption underneath says: GARBAGE GUTS: Garvey Quinn shows he can really pack it away.

I'm not the main attraction on the page, though. The bigger picture is Seagrave coming out of the courtroom after the ruling, smiling, and giving the finger to the cameras. The huge headline just says, GET STUFFED! Later in the day when Stuie phones to rev me up about going to the premiere, he tells me the latest he's heard from his contact in Seagrave's office. It seems the old pisspot judge who made the ruling watched the whole of the private screening with one hand down his trousers, and said it was the most fun he'd had in years.

On Friday night, when the limo arrives, I hang back on the porch, not wanting to take the first step towards it, but Dad nudges me into action.

Come on son, he says. You wanted to be an actor, and this is where it's led you. I don't care about those pissant interviews, you can dodge them, but when your real acting work's up on the screen, you got to get out there and take responsibility, take it on the chin. Otherwise, what's the point of your life?

I don't know, I say.

I squeeze inside the limo, and then Dad fits himself in beside me as best he can, and my brother Dean gets in the front. They're coming along to look after me, but I wish they weren't, they're even less equipped to cope with this than I am, and it's only going to hurt.

Don't worry son, Dad says. We'll protect you from that pack of bastards, but you've got to hold your head up high.

Yeah, says Dean. Whatever the job might have been like, you did it to the best of your ability, and no one's got the right to kick your arse for that.

When we arrive at the State theatre the mob's already there, the red carpet and the crowd barriers and the photographers, and I wish the limo could keep going and drop me round the back, let me sneak in in the dark once the film's underway. Some hope, though – Seagrave and his henchmen really put the pressure on, they spelled it out to me, you're the star of this movie and you've got to make your entrance. As I wobble from the car, I hear the same gasp of disbelief I got when I came out from behind the curtains in the TV studio, as if people who've only seen pictures of me aren't quite prepared for the reality of just how big I really am. The flashes are going off all around, and I try to keep from looking at them, just keep walking, Dad on one side of me, my brother on the other, in their rented dinner suits. If I can just get into the crowd inside, the throng of first nighters already milling around with champagne glasses, I'll be less in view of the cameras.

Inside, though, it's not much better. There are still plenty of media around, they just have to get in closer for the shots they want. Seagrave greets me, obviously for the benefit of the TV camera that's aimed at us, a big smile and a slap on the back.

Garvey, fantastic to see you here. Hey, this is it, after all our hard work, here's the payoff. He turns round to snap at a waiter. Hey, you, get Mr Quinn a champagne. Now!

Dad's staying close, and he calls out, yeah, and we'll have some too.

While the champagne's coming, Seagrave turns to the TV crew, points at me, and says to the interviewer, isn't he great? Isn't he fantastic? I mean, is this dedication to a role, or what? Garvey Quinn is one of a kind.

Very impressive indeed, says the man with the microphone. So how do you feel about all this, Garvey? Any regrets?

Don't know, really.

The interviewer must have seen me on the chat show, and knows that's about all he's going to get out of me, so he turns back to Seagrave.

Stirling Seagrave, perhaps you can tell us, where's Bryan Mars?

How would I know?

The interviewer persists, we heard that he was going to at last come out of hiding to attend the premiere.

Who the hell told you that?

At that moment there's some excitement outside, and the crew turns away to catch it. I can see that Madeleine's arriving, the one person I can't bear to face because she alone knows just how badly I stuffed up. She's on the arm of Johnny Hearn, and he's the one they all want to see, in no time there's a mob around him. I hear he's become really famous these days, though I wouldn't know, I've got no interest in who's doing what anymore. Seagrave glares across the room, looking for someone.

GARVEY QUINN

I ask Seagrave, what's this about Bryan Mars being here?

He answers without looking at me, we talked about it at one stage, then we decided it wasn't worth the trouble. I mean, can you remember how useless the guy was when we went to see him? Maybe you caught it from him. Hey, you, get your arse over here!

I see that the person he's summoning is the publicity lady, sweaty and maybe a bit pissed, with her black skirt now scrunched up to about half its length. She comes over, looking worried. Yes, Stirling, what is it?

I just had Larry Rinehart asking me why Bryan Mars wasn't here, like he was expected. How the fuck did he know?

Sorry Stirling, before you went cold on the Bryan idea, I leaked it to a couple of selected reporters, ones I knew I could trust, so they'd be ready to really exploit the angle when it happened.

You leaked it? I told you it was meant to be a fucking secret!

So it is true, I say to Seagrave. You were going to have both of us here together. Both of us looking like this.

Yeah, well, that's how you look, isn't it? And it's not like you didn't get paid for your trouble.

I tell him, I went through all this to play a part, not to be in a freak show.

I hired you, and you'll do what I damn well want you to do!

Dad and my brother step in. You watch what you say to him or you'll answer to us. We're family and we don't care who you are, you wanker, they'll be scraping you off the pavement!

Seagrave moves away fast, over to meet Madeleine and Johnny Hearn. I try to keep well away, I don't want to talk to her, what could I say?, and I don't want to be photographed anywhere near her, don't want to give people any extra questions to think about, like who'd believe fatso used to shag this beautiful girl who's now bonking the hottest thing in Hollywood. But once Seagrave is caught up in Hollywood bullshit talk with Johnny Hearn, Madeleine comes over anyway, and touches my arm. Her touch used to be the most beautiful thing in the world, but now I shrink from her.

Well, she says. Now we get to see whether it was all worth it.

I don't answer, I can't bear to look at her, I did this and lost her and now I just wish she'd go away and not remind me. But somehow she seems determined to make this into some big moment, standing right up close, almost close enough to kiss me if my stomach wasn't in the way.

It's all right if you say it wasn't worth it, she tells me, and despite myself, I look into her beautiful clear eyes, and keep trying not to look down to her body, so perfectly squeezed into her shiny red dress she looks like she's stepped out of a mould.

She goes on, I understand, you don't have to pretend anymore, it's your own truth that matters.

Dad's not having any of this, and he waves a finger at her.

Make yourself scarce, girlie, don't you have respect for anyone's feelings? Piss off back to Hollywood, as far as I'm concerned they're welcome to you.

I'm sorry Mr Quinn, I'm sorry you feel like that, and I want you to know that I still have the greatest respect for –

Then Dad says, fucking bloody hell, but not at Madeleine. He's charging over to the main door where two more arrivals are coming in, nobody the media are interested in, but the centre of Dad's attention. It's Mum, walking in holding hands with the lighting designer she ran off with, or ex-lighting designer these days. Now they live in Byron Bay, making sort of New Age jewellery, and it comes back to me that ages ago Stuie had passed on a query from the producers about who I wanted to invite. Dean rushes over too, like he's wanting to keep things calm, because Dad's shouting, how can you show your face? Look what they've done to my son! I hold you personally responsible, people like you are the scum of the earth!

I'm worried that Dad, after barely holding himself back from slugging Seagrave, is now about to really let loose and take his anger out on the lighting designer, who looks like he wants to run and hide, and Mum's saying, please Ken, not on your son's big night. And then –

It's Bryan Mars, it's Bryan Mars!

Dad, and everyone else, stops dead. Out on the street, this bloke is making the biggest entrance of the night. At first I can't see properly because of the crowd, but even when I do get a proper look, I can't quite take it in, because he's slim and graceful, and his hair looks just like mine did in the first stages of filming, just like Bryan Mars in fact. And he's waving and smiling, this sort of glowing smile, and people are waving back, Bryan, great to see you, fantastic, and there are little bursts of applause.

As Bryan Mars approaches the doors, Seagrave pushes past me, over to a security guard. Keep that fucker out of here, he's not invited, Seagrave says, but the security guard doesn't seem to get the message, and a moment later the publicity lady goes up to him, sounding breathless.

Mr Mars, so glad you could make it. Look, I'm sorry, when we thought you weren't coming, we re-allocated your seat, but you can have mine.

She hands over a ticket.

Thank you so much. You're very kind.

StUffED

Bryan Mars is soon lost in a sea of wellwishers, and I hear Seagrave go to the publicity lady and snarl at her, you're done for, bitch.

I couldn't give a shit, she tells him. That's Bryan Mars. Next to him, you're nothing.

A bell rings, and we're being ushered in. Soon I'll be in the dark, at least not so visible, but somehow Bryan Mars catches up with me, grabs my arm, still smiling.

Garvey, it's good to see you again. Look, no hard feelings, I want you to know that, I understand. Hey, I think I'm really going to enjoy this.

Inside, they've removed an armrest beween two seats, specially for me, but even with the double width, it's still a tight fit. As the lights go down and the curtains pull apart, I'm kicking myself for not bringing something to eat, something to get me through this.

The first thing that comes on is a close-up shot of me and Madeleine going hard at it on the stack of towels on the floor of the change room, and by the sound of Madeleine's squeal it's the take where she didn't have to do any acting, and neither did I. I know my dick's only just out of view, and so's Duncan Young, but thankfully the camera stays close in, at least this time. Then the picture wobbles a bit, and fades, and a shot of me in the Darwin house gradually comes into focus, me as I look now, my hand in a king-size KFC bucket, so it's meant to look as if Bryan's in the present, thinking about what he's lost. My voice comes on, one of those voice-overs I did, I'm saying, minute after minute, hour after hour, day after day, month after month, year after year, all I do is stuff my face and think of those moments with Vicki. Those moments, lost in her, when everything seemed possible.

At that point I'm shown shoving another chicken nugget

into my mouth, which is already nearly full, and giving my groin a rub. That's when I hear the laugh, a honking, hooting blast from down the front. Other people react to it as well, and someone asks, who on earth is that laughing? An answer comes quickly enough.

That's Bryan Mars.

And that's how it goes for the whole ninety minutes of this stupid, pointless movie for which I've totally fucked up my life, the real Bryan Mars's laughter dominating everything. The swimming, the record breaking, the days of glory, are got out of the way in minutes, mostly shown as a background to Bryan and Vicki's insatiable sex life. When we get to the rescue, that awful tank scene where I punched out the shark prompts Bryan's biggest guffaw yet. After that come scenes of the decline, the camera lingering on my increasing flesh, shot from angles that make me look like a giant slug. And all through, intercutting the punch-ups and the failures and the humiliations are these flashback scenes of me and Madeleine rooting like crazy, over and over again, shrieking and grunting for all we're worth, until Bryan the blob comes on again, up in Darwin with his hand down his enormous trousers. I hear somebody near me whisper, you wouldn't think he could even find it anymore, and maybe that's what Bryan's thinking too, because from down the front, his laughter just keeps on coming. At least Bryan likes it, says someone near me, as we listen to more of that awful voice-over, oh, Vicki, remember in the shower you'd hold onto the towel rail and I'd give it to you doggy style, Oh, Vicki, Vicki, and then we fade into me and Madeleine doing exactly that, and I wonder where she's sitting, what she's feeling about all this.

After the faked suicide scene, when I'm shown waking up starkers on the beach, lying on my back with the family jewels in full view, Dad jumps up from the seat next to me.

StUffED

I've had all I can take, he says, without trying to keep his voice down. I've made allowances for you, but there's only so far a bloke can go, and I'm not having any sympathy for a pervert. You're on your own now.

Dad leaves, and Dean goes with him, and the movie just goes on and on, and Bryan Mars just goes on and on laughing.

★ ★ ★

BRYAN MARS

When you come out afterwards everyone's coming up to you and acting like you need sympathy, so you keep having to tell them, it's all right, don't worry. The one who looks like he needs sympathy is that poor actor, you've never seen anyone look so embarrassed, except maybe yourself in pictures they took after you'd fallen in the pool at the Olympics. Garvey Quinn didn't get anywhere near that expression in the movie, but he's got it now, and everybody's avoiding him, like they're worried they'll catch something from him, failure, you suppose, despair and lies.

They all want to be your friend, though, they all want to know, Bryan, what was so funny? You do your best to tell them, even though you're not quite sure yourself, you're still trying to put a label on it. You come out with something like, I suppose it was seeing what somebody had made of my life, seeing how little had got through. I'd spent so long looking on my life as a tragedy, but they'd seen it as a cartoon.

A pretty explicit cartoon, someone tells you.

Oh, the sex scenes, you say to them. They didn't do that to me, they did it to that poor bloke going out the door. As you say it, they turn round to look at Garvey Quinn dragging himself out, and you hope they've at least given him a limo to get home in, you hope they haven't just dumped him. You want to run over to him and say, look mate, somehow it can get better, believe me. You don't of course, you're surrounded, wanted like never before, even when you were breaking records. Already you're fielding offers, chat shows, newspapers, radio, too much for a night like this so you tell them, phone me in the morning and you give them your new mobile number. You've got nothing to fear, so you give them the address of your new flat as well, you rented it just that morning, you said to the agent, I'll round up some references as soon as I can, and he said, but you're Bryan Mars, you don't need references.

Then for a moment you find you're not the only centre of attention. They've all turned to watch that actress, the one who played Vicki, who's just coming out, I think her name's Madeleine something-or-other. She was about the best thing in it, she could actually swim, but right now you see that she's in tears, her hair's gone stringy and her make-up's running down her face. She's holding onto this guy who's telling people to get out of the fucking way, arsehole, and most of them take notice, except a photographer who gets too close just outside the doorway and gets slammed, his camera trampled on. Security guards are running, there's a scuffle and the poor actress is screaming, you see her run off into the night and you wonder if she'll meet up with Garvey Quinn, who must still be out there. You wonder how well they know each other, considering what they had to do to each other in the film. Some of those scenes looked so real, and you could swear that just for the tiniest split second they let you glimpse him with a hard-on, dipping into her, but you know they can fake just about anything these days in movies.

You're ready to go, it's been a long couple of days, and when things have quietened down and the crowd's back around you, you tell people, nice meeting you all, be bound to speak to you again soon, I think I've had about enough excitement for one day. Right away you get offers of lifts, everybody's only too happy to drive you, wait here while I bring the Merc round the front, Bryan, but you say, thanks anyway, very nice of you, but I feel like the walk. You haven't taken a step, though, when Stirling Seagrave pushes through the mob, looking crazy with anger, and starts shouting at you.

You bastard, you smart-arsed bastard, well let me tell you nobody puts something like that over Stirling Seagrave and gets away with it. You rain on my parade, fucker, and you pay for it! You'll wish you'd stayed right where you were.

You want to say to him, would the movie have been any better or worse if I hadn't come? But he doesn't give you the chance, just stamps off. You've got some idea he's not finished with you yet, but you're not too worried, you know you've got his measure, just the way you could always tell when you looked around at the field as you lined up on the blocks.

You get a great night's sleep, and then the phone starts ringing, and within minutes you've pretty well got the day booked up, just like it was sometimes in the old days, though back then you had somebody else doing it for you. This is much better, arranging it yourself, you feel like you can keep it under control.

First off you're taken to talk to Russell Hackshaw, one of the Mr Bigs in radio. You remember him from before, you talked to him a couple of times, but then you were just a kid. He was there last night, and he gives his listeners a bit of background.

Last night a movie premiered, not just any movie, but the long awaited *Fish Out of Water*, the amazing story of Bryan Mars, someone whose ups and downs have given many of us food for thought over the years. And, ladies and gentlemen, it makes me sad to have to say this, but that movie is an absolute stinker, and so is the lead performance, you'd have to say it's the most gross, indulgent, sexually immature and downright disgusting piece of filth ever to appear in a cinema. The so-called wonderboy director Stirling Seagrave has put together what looks like a porno version of *The Three Stooges*, but without the jokes, and as for that once promising young actor Garvey Quinn, he's going to have to live with his conscience for the rest of his life. He's going to forever have to ask himself, how could I have done such a thing? If you haven't already got the message ladies and gentlemen, what I'm saying is, on no account should you go and see this movie.

But, thankfully, there was one ray of light in last night's otherwise grim experience, and that was the unexpected presence of Bryan Mars himself. Confronted by this revolting picture of himself, Bryan behaved with a good humour and generosity of spirit that was an inspiration to us all, a reminder that even in the face of the utmost depravity and degradation, human dignity will ultimately triumph. And it's my enormous pleasure to have Bryan with me now. Bryan Mars, welcome back.

Thank you very much. It's a pleasure to be here. And thank you very much for such kind words.

They're heartfelt, believe me. Bryan, let's get right down to the important things, shall we, because there's a lot about your story that needs filling in, a lot of questions to be answered.

That's fine by me.

No doubt many of our listeners will have seen you in this morning's newspapers and saw the way you look and thought, what was all the fuss about? So why do you think people saw you that way, when you were first sighted? Were they lying?

No, Russell, I don't believe they were lying. I believe people tell the truth as they see it. And I suppose people find it hard to let go the image they last had of you. They see what they expect to see. But I don't hold that against them.

And Stirling Seagrave's willingness to seize on that gross image of you, to base his film on it? How do you feel about what he's done?

He made the film he wanted to make. He expressed his own personal view of the world, and I've got no worries with anybody doing that. And I mean, it's just a movie, it's not like it was a matter of life and death.

Life and death Bryan. That gets us into an area we can't dodge any longer. Bryan, what really happened? The day you disappeared? Did you ever really mean to kill yourself?

Oh yes. Definitely.

So, why didn't you?

You realise you're not quite ready to answer this one. If you understood that, you'd probably understand a lot of other things as well. You need some more thinking time, but you remember from when you did radio before, allowing yourself time to think is a problem, they don't like silences, you have to give them something to go on with, just enough.

That's a hard one. It's a question I've struggled with for a long time. What I remember is that I was struggling to force myself under water. I'd swum as far out as I could, and I was out of condition by that stage so I was exhausted, and I'd thought, now it'll just happen, I'll be pulled under and I'll die. But, something was stopping me.

And what was that, Bryan?

Partly, I think, it was that I was pretty big by that stage. And you might think a fat man would be heavier, so he'd sink more easily, but in fact it's the reverse, you become more buoyant.

So in fact the thing that made you want to kill yourself was also the thing that was keeping you alive.

Being fat wasn't what made me want to kill myself. It was the emptiness. The nothingness. By that stage I was just longing for a sense of non-being.

Gee, Bryan, we're getting into some pretty heavy philosophical territory here, aren't we? I wonder if we could just stay with you in the water a bit longer, at your moment of truth.

No worries. So I was out there in the water, struggling to go under, yet somehow the water wouldn't take me. I think there was some part of me refusing to do this. You see, I'd always felt so at home in the water, I'd spent half my life in the water, and when you think about it, we humans are mostly water, anyway, aren't we? I mean, after all, life came out of the sea, and I was part of that life. I felt suddenly, strongly connected to it again, and the nature of life is to go on, not to annihilate itself.

I think I see where you're coming from, Bryan.

The real turning point was when I realised there were fish swimming around me. I felt I was one of them, and I mean, people used to call me the fish. I found myself keeping pace with them, despite my lack of condition, I wanted to swim.

You wanted to swim? As simple as that?

Yes. As simple as that.

We're going to have to wind this up soon, but can you just tell us, what happened in the end? Did you get washed up on a beach, like in the movie?

No, the fish and I all ended up in a trawling net together. When the fishermen hauled me out they got the shock of their lives, but they didn't have a clue who I was. Anyway, they warmed me up, and one of them was as big as me so they gave me some of his spare gear. They were illegals, and they might have been worried the Navy would be out searching for me, because they just kept going until they got to the Northern Territory. Then they put me ashore on a quiet bit of coastline.

Yours is a remarkable story, Bryan, and I'd happily talk to you all day about it, but sadly we're going to have to wind things up. It's been an honour having you in here, an absolute inspiration. Thank you Bryan Mars.

And thank you Russell, the pleasure's all mine.

You're pleased with how it went, by and large, considering you'd never really thought any of those things before. When you get back to your flat, though, pretty well straight away, there's two policemen there, they've come to take you back to the station so charges can be laid, though they're pretty apologetic about it.

Sorry to have to do this to you, Mr Mars, and my mum will kill me if she finds out it was me arresting you, one of them says. We heard you on the radio before, in the divvy van, jeeze you were good. Sounds like the movie's shit, but.

Word's obviously got around, because when the divvy van pulls up at the police station, there are camera crews waiting. You give them a wave and a smile, and then a couple of old ladies call out to the police, let him go, you mongrels, let Bryan go. You turn to them, and you tell them, don't worry, everything's going to be all right.

Inside, the detective laying the charges is just as apologetic. He tells you, if it was up to us, we'd just let the whole thing drop, but some concerned citizen has seen fit to draw the matter to our attention and there's not much we can do, though if I ever meet him in a dark alley, I won't be responsible. You know it must be Seagrave, this is his revenge – the company's lawyers covered up for you before, and now they've dropped you right in it. You find yourself charged with creating a public mischief, and they also want to recover the costs involved in searching for you, helicopter fuel bills and such. When you leave, the cameras catch you again, and you give another wave or two.

The police drive you home. You say you don't mind walking, but they're only too happy to help out. On the way, nearly there, you pass a sports store, and you tell them, this'll be fine, right here, I've got a bit of shopping to do. You buy a tracksuit and some running shoes, some swimming goggles and one of those full length body suits everybody seems to race in now. It'll keep the loose folds of skin out of view until you get the chance to book in and have something done about it, maybe find a clinic in some country where nobody knows you. While you're in the shop you sign a couple of posters they drop in front of you, your hand goes onto automatic pilot, just the way it used to.

You've got some TV to do a bit later today, so as soon as you get home you change into the gear and head for the park that's not too far away. You want to fit in a trip to the nearest pool, but with all your commitments, a jog is all you can manage for now. You're not doing much more than a shuffle, but you feel so much freer than you did moving back and forth around that flat, up and down the balcony, and you know it'll come. Other runners, real runners, slow down to keep pace with you, they offer handshakes, good to meet you Bryan, good on you. Everybody must know you're here, because when you come out of the park gates, on the run home, there's another camera crew waiting. The reporter's got something to tell you, and they want a reaction.

The charges have been dropped. Alexander Morton put

a top team of QCs onto it right away, and they shot the case full of holes.

Well, that's really fantastic. I'm very grateful.

And Alexander Morton's also offered to pay all the rescue costs. How does that make you feel?

Alexander Morton's a very fine man. Look, thanks a lot for telling me that, I really appreciate it.

You jog home, and as you change you wonder if you should phone Alexander Morton and thank him, but something's holding you back. You realise you're not quite ready to talk to him. Not until you've said what you've got to say in this next interview, the one where they can see you.

★ ★ ★

GarVEY QUiNN

I'd put together a shopping list for Dad, yesterday morning, while I was trying to keep my mind off having to go to the premiere, just for something to do. It was just the usual stuff, ham, pork, sausages, bacon, and as many different cheeses as he could find on the display shelves, I don't like to saddle Dad with anything you can't easily pick up at Woolies, I know adventurous stuff freaks him out. But today the shopping list is still there, Dad didn't take it with him when he left for work, the way he usually does, and I suppose he's never going to again. You're on your own now son, was what he said, and it looks like he's going to keep to that. I'm not even sure he wants me in the house anymore, but I don't know what else to do except sit here until the food runs out, and after that consider my options, if I turn out to have any.

Fortunately the place is well stocked, I always put stuff on the shopping list long before we ran out of it, so the freezer's full of beef and pork and chickens and ducks, and there's piles of cheese and eggs and ham and bacon, plus sacks of potatoes. If I put it on the list, Dad would buy it, didn't bat an eyelid, anything to keep me from sneaking out again and getting spotted, and the cost didn't worry him because it was coming out of my bank account. I don't know what my balance is like now, I must have eaten a couple of truckloads since I came back home.

So there's a lot of food, but, on the other hand, there's not so much that I can't already visualise coming to the end of it. When I'm cooking one meal, and especially when I'm eating it, I'm already starting to think of the next couple of meals ahead, mentally weighing up how much is going to go into them, and then into me. And I know, at this rate, by about the middle of next week I'll be getting frantic.

The phone's rung a few times, and surprisingly, considering how I performed in the run-up to the premiere, people are wanting to set me up for some more public appearances. What they want, though, is for me to appear alongside the real Bryan Mars, and I'm not having a bar of that, no way. I know just how it would go, he'd be happy and smiling and magnanimous, there's something about him now, a sort of glow about him as if he's found out something that none of the rest of us know. I could tell that last night, and then this morning I heard him on the radio after Stuie phoned up and told me I ought to listen. I heard as much as I could take before I turned him off, and he was coming out with more of this stuff. And he goes on about how people must have seen him as fat when he got sprung in Darwin because that was the image they already had, but I know that's bullshit because I saw him up in Darwin, and he was just as bad as me. Worse, he's saying it doesn't matter about the movie, it's all OK, what people say about you doesn't matter, however disgusting it is, like he was Jesus Christ or somebody.

So I can see just how it would go, with me appearing alongside him, me looking like this and feeling like shit, and the interviewer would be saying, well Garvey Quinn, how can you justify doing this to yourself to play Bryan Mars, when we can all now see what Bryan's really like? The true answer would be, because the director told me to and I'm completely fucking stupid, but I know I wouldn't say that. I'd probably just mumble, don't know really, um, er, not sure, um, sorry, and hundreds of thousands of people would be watching me and thinking, that guy's a waste of space. A lot of space.

So it's definitely not going to happen, any appearances by me, and even if I'd been thinking about it, one of this morning's phone calls, from Seagrave, would have knocked that on the head. All he said was, if you make any public comment to anyone, so help me I'll murder you. I know people often say that sort of thing, but he sounded like he meant it.

Later, when Stuie comes round, I find out just how much shit Seagrave's really in. It's just started raining, and Stuie's a bit bedraggled, and big raindrops have made a pattern on his pale cream suit. He sits down by the kitchen bench and watches me cook, though when I give him a plate of blue cheese and salami chunks, he just picks at it, he's too interested in talking.

Last week, when Seagrave got the injunction lifted, that was just round one, Stuie tells me. The word is that Vicki and the pole vaulter are about to launch another attack. They're going to challenge the competence of that judge, and they're going to set out to show that Seagrave deliberately distorted what he knew to be the truth.

But that's his job, I say. He makes movies.

Yes, says Stuie. Only this time he picked the wrong target. Those two have got people in the highest places on their side. I hear even the attorney-general's sticking his oar in, in the interests of international goodwill. And with the groundswell that's building up against that movie, I'd say Seagrave's well and truly stuffed. And so is *Fish Out of Water* – that premiere could be the last time it's ever screened.

I sit down at the bench with my plate of spare ribs, and

ask whether Bryan Mars is involved in the lawsuit now, seeing as he's portrayed as being only interested in his dick and where the next feed's coming from.

No, Stuie tells me. It seems that they approached him, but he says he doesn't bear any malice towards anyone, and anyway it's only a movie.

Smug bastard.

He's on the box tonight, Dermot Prickle's interviewing him. I know you hate all this, but I think you better watch anyway, keep yourself up with the situation. You're still involved in it, whether you like it or not.

At that point, if I had the energy, if I could move fast enough, and I wasn't so busy with my spare ribs, I'd get up and hit him.

Yes Stuie, I fucking know I'm involved in it, whether I like it or not.

He looks surprised by my anger, though I can't imagine why.

Garvey, I'm only trying to look after your interests.

That really gets me going. I remember the conversation I had with him just after Seagrave had offered me the job.

Yeah, Stuie, looking after my interests like when Seagrave first offered me the job, and I told him I'd think about it. Jesus, you were practically frothing at the mouth, and you told me, you turn this down you might never work again because nobody else would want to hire somebody that stupid. Well, Stuie, I didn't turn it down, but I sure as hell won't ever work again, will I?

Every other agent in the business would have told you the same. Nobody could have predicted that Seagrave would go over the top like that. And, to be blunt, nor could they have predicted that you wouldn't have the discipline to get yourself back in shape when it was all over. People did try to help you you know, they fulfilled their obligations.

I don't want to hear anymore, I get enough reminders from everything that happens about what a hopeless joke I am, and I don't need it from Stuie as well.

Just go away, Stuie, if that's all you've got to tell me. Leave me alone.

One day you'll see things differently, says Stuie. At least I hope so. He reminds me one more time not to forget to watch Bryan Mars being interviewed on Dermot Prickle's show, and then he leaves. I just have time to cook up some bacon and eggs, the spare ribs weren't nearly enough, and then it's time for the show, time for even more of Bryan Mars.

Dermot Prickle gets the chit chat out of the way quickly, how wonderful it is that Bryan's back, what a load of crap the movie is, and as he does his usual, it's very kind of you to say so, Bryan keeps smiling that smile. When the camera pans over the audience, you can see he's got them eating out of his hand, they're ready to believe anything. Then Prickle brings it round to the serious stuff, the disappearance, and the apparent suicide.

You've already admitted that you really did mean to kill yourself when you swam out that day, but then you had some sort of spiritual experience with the fish, which made you want to go on living. Is it possible for you to tell us more about that moment, Bryan? Because many of us search for meaning, but few find it as clearly as you apparently did.

Then, for the first time, I see that smile go, instead he's looking serious, almost worried, like he's thinking something over. Prickle doesn't interrupt, and the camera stays right close in on his face, and he's given more quiet thinking time than anyone I've ever seen on television. Then finally the smile comes back halfway, and he gives his answer.

It wasn't just the fish. It was the shark. I told it I was sorry.

StUffED

There's a gasp from the audience, is this guy losing his marbles or what?, and Prickle stares at Bryan for a long moment before he manages to say the obvious.

You told a shark you were sorry?

Not just any shark. The shark.

Bryan now does his talking directly to the camera, not trying to have a chat with Dermot Prickle at all, like he's taken over the show.

I'm about to say something important, Bryan starts off. And if I'm treading on anybody's toes saying what I'm going to say, well, I'm sorry about that. When I rescued those people on the beach, yes, it's true, I did all that swimming, that was easy, because that was what I was good at. But the shark. The one I fought off. I have something to say about it. It was this big.

Now Bryan holds his hands apart. Not much wider apart than his shoulders. What he's showing is a shark just slightly larger than the big flathead Dad caught up on the Hawkesbury a few years ago, with a five-pound handline and a frozen prawn.

It was this big, Bryan repeats. It was a tiddler. And I ripped its eye out.

Dermot Prickle, and the audience, look dumbfounded, though I'm remembering the funny feeling I had about the size of the fake shark they had me fighting in the tank, Jaws Jnr. Then Prickle gets himself together.

But Bryan, other people who were there that day attested to how huge that shark was. And Alexander Morton was right next to you in the water and he said afterwards he thought it was going to swallow both of you.

Bryan does another one of his long thinking stares, straight at the camera, and once again they let him get away with it.

Yes, Bryan finally answers. Alexander Morton did say that. And Mr Morton, if you're watching this, I mean no disrespect to you sir, but when you said that, that was the beginning of my downfall.

You can see Dermot Prickle reacting to something on his autocue, because he says, Bryan, if I can just interrupt you there, this might be a good time to remind our viewers of exactly what was said that day, about your extraordinary actions.

The producers must have been well prepared to re-run clips of the real Bryan Mars story if they needed to, and there's that news footage taken on the beach shortly after the rescue, by the first crew on the scene. Bryan's in the background, just a few feet away, exhausted, gasping for breath, completely done in after all his swims back and forth to the shipwreck, with a medic trying to throw a blanket round him. In the foreground, though, is Alexander Morton, in the remains of his dinner suit, sitting on the tray of a surf rescue truck, having a few puffs of oxygen. It's a clip I remember seeing at the time it happened, and then again when they showed us a lot of news footage in the lead-up to filming. Morton's a big powerfully built man, once a football star, but these days showing signs of a few too many big deal lunches with his TV executives. In the movie, Charlie Wainscott, an ex-wrestler and one of Duncan Young's old pisshead actor mates, played Morton, though I think Morton himself does it better.

This young man is the ultimate hero, Morton says on the newsclip. What he did was truly superhuman. When I saw the size of that shark, I was sure we were both going to die. It was as big as. As big as.

Then you wait for him to find the right comparison, until he says, it was as big as that surfboat over there. No, bigger.

StUffED

Then the news cameraman does a quick pan across to the surf club boat that had come along too late to help with the rescue, then back to Morton, but on the way, in the background, I notice something I hadn't spotted before. You get a glimpse of Bryan Mars looking over, and he's looking surprised, amazed even, and he's moving his mouth like he's about to say something. I suppose I should have spotted it before, because that's the sort of detail actors are meant to use to build up a character, but somehow that one went through to the keeper. Bryan doesn't get to say anything though, because then Alexander Morton's off again.

Bryan Mars pitted himself against a monster from the deep, Morton says. He drew upon reserves of courage that I never believed possible, and which I will remember until my dying day. He is a truly great man, and I know that that greatness will go on to be rewarded by far more than the pile of Olympic gold medals he will win next year. Bryan Mars, I salute you.

Then you glimpse Bryan again, not trying to say anything now, just shrugging as if to say, come on, it was nothing much really. Then Prickle puts the question.

So, Bryan, you're saying that Alexander Morton lied.

He exaggerated. Considerably. As I say, the shark was this big. He holds up his hands again, and by now the shark seems to have shrunk to about the size of a half stick of French bread.

We could have just swum past it, Bryan goes on, sounding like he might even be going to cry. I just saw something flash in front of me, saw some teeth and just instinctively lashed out and got my thumb right in its eye. I watched it swim away, writhing in pain, and it was all so unnecessary.

Bryan, you'd just rescued ten people in a wild sea. By any standards, that made you a hero.

But I did not fight a giant shark! This is the first time he's raised his voice, shown real anger. Then his voice goes calm. From then on, I was known for something you can't measure. Swimming you can measure with the stopwatch, you either do it or you don't. But this was the sort of thing that turns into legend. It gets passed down over generations.

More and more I'm thinking Bryan Mars is a bullshit artist of the first order, but it's obvious no one in the studio feels like this. Prickle asks him, at the time, you didn't feel you could challenge Alexander Morton's account of things?

How could I? I was just a young swimmer.

But you're challenging it now?

I've lived a lot since then.

Somehow Prickle works the interview back to the shark, the real one, because saying sorry to a shark has obviously still got some mileage in it.

Bryan, let me get this straight, are you saying that when you went out there to try to drown yourself, the shark you encountered was the very same shark you encountered on the day of the rescue?

It was the same size. It had the same markings. It had an injury to its eye.

And you just told it you were sorry. Just like that.

Bryan gets into his thinking expression for a moment.

I honestly believe it felt my regret. And at what was meant to be the moment of my death, I felt its life.

Luckily, before we get any more of this stuff, Prickle is reacting to another signal

Bryan, the producer tells me that Alexander Morton has phoned through. He wants to speak to you. Publicly, if that's all right with you.

That's fine by me.

Then this voice seems to come out of a speaker, the way

they're all looking up to it, Alexander Morton saying, Bryan, I said those things about you and the shark because I was so awestruck by your actions, I lost all sense of proportion. I suppose when you're in the presence of greatness you lose your sense of proportion. But I had no idea of the burden that would place on you. And I want you to know I'm sorry. I'm truly sorry.

Mr Morton, it means a great deal to me that you've called. I appreciate it.

You never stopped being a hero, Bryan.

So it's sorry all round. Bryan said sorry to the baby shark, now Alexander Morton's said sorry to him, and I'm sorry I ever heard of Bryan Mars, I'm sorry the shark wasn't big enough to eat him. If I had a gun right now I'd do an Elvis and shoot the television, but instead I just kill it with the remote, and it's only about a minute after that that the phone rings. When I find it's that journo Len Buckler on the other end, I'm sort of pleased, and I find myself saying to him, nice to hear from you again, Len, Mate, what would you like to talk about?

* * *

BRYAN MARS

As you dive in, the cameras are watching your every move. There are cameras all over the place, at both ends of the pool, along the sides, underwater, on top, in fact just about as many as you'd have covering the Olympics. They're all from the one crew, you've given the channel exclusive rights to cover your return to the pool, they seem to be working up a few projects that look like being good for you, so you decide you might as well ride with them. On the other hand, when they said they didn't want the public looking on, that's where you drew the line. You told them, you've got exclusive coverage, but if anybody's interested enough to come along and see me have my first swim, I'm not going to deny them that right. They didn't argue, either, which is something you've been noticing lately. You just have to say what you want, and people will say, sure Bryan, that's fine, whatever you want, you've got it.

Not that this really is your first time back in the pool. Last couple of nights you'd sneaked out, over to the old Aquatic Centre, timed it so you'd be there when everyone else was leaving. And you found some things never change, because, as always, Arthur Snow was the last one there, and just as he was locking up the old rusty gate at the side entrance they use, you went up to him and you said, can I come in Arthur?

StUffED

Arthur just looked at you, didn't say anything more than, all right Bryan. So there you were, back on the tiles, the smell of chlorine all around you and the filtration pumps humming, and you got out of your tracksuit, stood up on the block, and in you went, your first dive, breaking the water as cleanly as a dolphin. You stayed underwater a long time, as far as your momentum could carry you, before you came up and looked for your stroke. You tried it, one two three four breathe, and you got it right away, the power wasn't there yet, your muscles not nearly as strong as they were, but you moved as easily as ever. After four laps you came up for a moment, and Arthur was still there, watching.

He just said to you, looks like you'll be all right. Could you pull the gate shut when you leave? Then he was gone, and you kicked away from the end, swam off into the dark, all the pool lights out, one two three four breathe.

So now, as you get ready for what everybody thinks is your first time back, you've already had that first, tentative session, and then another one last night. Last night's was a real swim, thirty laps, beautiful, and you felt like you could have gone on forever, but you didn't want to do too much too soon and risk muscle stiffness. There's a crowd, still gathering, quite a few hundred as you step out of your tracksuit and stand up on the block. You don't do any posing, any playing to the crowd, you're flying into the water virtually as soon as you've stepped up, taking them all by surprise, and just as you're going under you hear that little gasp from people, like you get just about every time you appear somewhere.

You've got the stroke going beautifully, even better than last night, so it was good you had that tune-up first, so no one's disappointed. You do swim virtually forever this time, lap after lap after lap, and wondering, if you just keep on swimming, will they all just keep on watching, forever and ever and ever? Your bet is they probably will.

Afterwards, while you're still in the middle of changing, you hear the ring of your mobile coming out of your gear bag. You get it out, tell whoever it is, hang on, and finish pulling your tracksuit back on, you've never liked being rushed when you're winding down after a swim. You find it's Alexander Morton on the phone, the second conversation you've had with him today, the first was over lunch, when he gave you a sort of general run through of how important it was that a career such as yours was managed correctly, there were doors open to you now that couldn't be ignored. You listened, and a lot of it made sense, and you figured that when you had someone as influential as him on your side, you might as well go with it. You more or less said yes to everything, and you could see that made him happy, somehow the guy seems hugely honoured just to know you.

This time, though, on the mobile, there's a worry in his voice. Something's coming out in one of the papers that could have an impact on your public image, he tells you. You need to see it right away.

You tell him, thanks, I'll run out and buy a copy as soon as I've finished changing, but he says, it's not on the stands yet, an inside source faxed me the page. You tell him, all right, do you want me to come to your office. No, he says, I'm in the car, right outside the pool.

Because of the tinted glass, you can't see anything inside the stretched Roller until a guy in a chauffeur's uniform swings a door open for you and gives a little bow as he does so. Inside, it's virtually an office, with a computer and a fax machine and God knows what else, along with the usual cocktail cabinet and mini fridge, you saw a bit of this stuff in the old days, so it's not a complete shock. Morton is sitting back, a serious frown on his big high bald man's forehead, and he waits until the door is closed before he shows you the squeezed down fax of the *Tele*'s front page. It says, Star tells: Bryan's a fraud!

I thought that fool was completely done for, the way he looked, Morton tells you. Someone must have put him up to this. You grab the page from him, and the second sheet that follows on from where it says, continued on page three. On the first page, along with that headline, are two pictures; one of Garvey Quinn, enormous, playing you, in a scene up in Darwin, wearing just a pair of huge flowery shorts, one hand down the front of them and the other shoving a chicken drumstick into his mouth; the other from the Dermot Prickle show, you looking relaxed, smiling and slim. Underneath there's another headline, in smaller type, that says, Which one's the big fat slug?

There's not much writing on the front page, all it says is, in an exclusive interview with Len Buckler, actor Garvey Quinn stood by his portrayal of Bryan Mars, saying that he played him as a bloated, sex-obsessed loser because that's exactly how he was when they met. Quinn claims that when he and the producers met Bryan in Darwin, the former swimming star was, quote, a huge fat slug, he was disgusting, and he just sat there stuffing Kentucky Fried Chicken into his mouth. He seemed really depressed.

You think, anyone would be depressed meeting those film makers. Morton is watching you as you read, and you turn over the page to where Garvey Quinn describes the moment where you were shown a photograph of your old girlfriend Vicki and you let out a bellow like a mad elephant and chased them out of the room, as if that's supposed to prove that the movie got it right, that you spent your whole day thinking about Vicki and tugging yourself blind. Whatever you might be like now, that's how you were then, he played you honestly, to the best of his abilities as an actor, what more could he do. And, he says, quote, that was a clever trick Bryan played on us, losing all that weight and turning up at the premiere, but that doesn't make the movie any less truthful. It was true to the reality of what we saw at the time.

You know, of course that the movie's big problem isn't whether it's truthful or not, its big problem is that it's crap. You look up at Morton and you tell him, don't worry, it's nothing I can't handle. But all the same, you're glad you've got someone like him on your side.

★ ★ ★

GaRVEY QUiNN

Maybe someone smarter than me would have known to record the interview, so afterwards they could be certain they really said the stuff that turns up in the paper. I'm not sure I said Bryan was a huge fat slug, I've got an idea Len Buckler used those words and I just sort of agreed. I'm not sure I said disgusting, either, though I did talk about the KFC and the picture of Vicki. But saying he tricked us? I don't think so. It makes me look like such an arsehole, here's the new sleek shining Bryan with the world eating out of his hand, and I'm saying it's not real, he just did it to embarrass us. Who are they going to believe, him or me? No wonder Dad just hurled the paper at me and said, why'd you do it, son, don't you know when to keep your trap shut for your own good? and stamped out of the house like he can't stand to be anywhere near me.

Just after Dad goes, I hear a car come by, pull up outside, and the next moment the front window smashes. I hit the floor, and wait until I hear the car move off before I drag myself up again to investigate. Someone's thrown a frozen chook through the window, a Steggles number 18, and I wonder for a moment whether I should thaw it out for lunch. There are more important things to consider, though, like staying alive, and I phone Stuie to see if he's got some advice, I don't think I'm going to be able to stay here, people must hate me. Stuie's not surprised to hear from me, in fact he says, I thought it might be you. You're about the only one of my clients I ever hear from these days.

I tell him, Stuie, I'm in danger, someone just threw a frozen chook through the window, and he says back to me, a frozen chook?, and I say, yeah, a Steggles number 18, and I hear a little stifled laugh. I tell him, Stuie, this isn't funny, next time it could be a bomb. Don't worry, he tells me, Stirling Seagrave's going to look after you.

Seagrave? what's he got to do with it? I ask.

Suddenly Stirling's your number one fan. You're his golden-haired boy after that interview. You might just turn out to be the producers' secret weapon when this mess goes to court.

I groan, oh no, but Stuie just tells me to pack my bag, Seagrave's car should be there any minute. I just hope it's not a stretch limo.

In fact it's a Hummer, one of those enormous four-wheel drive troop carriers like Arnold Schwarzenegger owns. We should be safe in this, Seagrave tells me, these things won the Gulf War. But for something so big, there's surprisingly little room, and I'm as cramped as I was in the WRX. Seagrave's wearing some kind of army surplus camouflage gear, though it would be hard for him to blend in with the bush because his hair's in bright gold dreadlocks. I ask him, where are we going?

Somewhere safe, he answers. I've borrowed an apartment for you in a high rise in Potts Point. There's a nice quiet back entrance and we'll take you up in the goods lift. We have to keep you out of harm's way until the court hearing. After that interview you gave, you're worth your weight in gold. Then he looks over at me. Well, maybe not quite that much.

I can't imagine why he thinks I'm going to go out of my

way to help him. I ask him, what do you want me to do?

You're going to be called to give evidence. Either by our side or theirs, it doesn't really matter. And what it's going to come down to is whether our movie truthfully represented Bryan as we saw him that time in Darwin. And we're going to be saying that Bryan told us a whole lot of stuff about the way he felt, and we took that in good faith when we made the movie.

I tell him, but that's bullshit. Why should I lie to help you?

Seagrave turns out to be one of those people whose driving goes to pieces as soon as they get angry, made more terrifying because it's just started raining. He floors the Hummer to try to get it through a gap opening up in the outside lane as we come up William Street towards the Cross, then slams the brakes on as the gap closes up. The big Hummer does a bit of a skid on the wet road, but even while he's trying to get it back under control, Seagrave's blasting the horn, which sounds like a prison camp hooter in a war movie.

Stupid fucking idiots, he shouts, and I'm probably included. He tells me, I've read the interview, you weren't lying then.

I didn't exactly say the stuff the way it came out in the newspaper, I tell him, in fact I wish I hadn't said anything at all. And I'm not going to get up in court and lie for anybody, as a matter of fact I think there's a law against it.

This gets him really mad, and he starts trying to intimidate some poor guy in a chopped-top Vee-Dub, ramming the Hummer right up behind and hitting the horn.

Move it, arsehole, he shouts, then to me says, you'll do what you're fucking told! Don't think you can just walk away from this, you're as much involved in the movie as anyone, you're going to be linked with it for the rest of your life, in fact all of us are, so don't you think it deserves a fight?

No I don't, I shout back at him. I think it's shit, and so does everybody else, and I don't know why you don't just let them bury it and save everybody further embarrassment!

By now we're right into Kings Cross, heading up Darlinghurst Road, which is a stupid way to be going when I'm supposed to be being kept under wraps, especially in the Hummer, which everybody would be staring at anyway, even if Seagrave wasn't driving like a complete psycho. The usual early evening crowd is out on the footpath, quite a few sit under cafe umbrellas, and I see faces turning to stare each time the Hummer does another lunge forward or lurches sideways. Seagrave hasn't mastered the complicated gear-change either, so the noise of grating gears gives the crowd one more reason to gawp.

So, Mr Soapie Actor, Seagrave shouts back at me, you think you're qualified to say my film is shit, do you, you think that just because I've made you a star, suddenly you have powers of artistic judgement!

It's the art bit that gets me going, never mind the sarcastic crap about my being a star, and I'm shouting just as loudly as he is, art doesn't come into it and it never has and you know it, you wanker, I've sat through enough hopeless movies to know that yours is about the worst one ever made! You're just an egomaniac who likes making people do degrading, humiliating things to put you in the big time.

Seagrave's just about screaming by now, you just don't get it, do you, and why would anybody expect you to, you're just a piece of meat, that's all you actors are, you're pieces of meat that I move around in front of a camera, and if you can't understand my vision, well too fucking bad, who asked you anyway?

I come back at him, yeah, I'm just a piece of meat and

my opinion isn't worth shit, and yet you expect me to get up in court and support your side of the story. Why would they take notice of me anyway?

By now we're coming up to the stretch of Darlinghurst Road where the bikies always leave a row of Harley-Davidsons parked front wheel out from the kerb. Seagrave dodges the Hummer round a taxi that's pulled up, then accelerates hard, shouting at me, they'll take notice of you if you say what you're told to say, the way you're told to say it, never mind thinking, leave that to others, it's not your job. Maybe that's why your performance sucked, the audience could see you thinking about what you were doing.

So, it sucked, did it? You reckon my performance sucked?

Yeah, he shouts, it sucked, it sucked big time. Maybe if I'd hired a real actor like Johnny Hearn, someone who could act fat as well as just look fat, we wouldn't be in this mess now.

This is the last straw, and I want to hit him, but his driving's dangerous enough already, he hasn't got the Hummer back under control after swerving round the taxi, and just as I shout, even if you'd cast Robert fucking de Niro the movie would have been a turkey, the back of the Hummer comes round and collects about eight of the Harley-Davidsons, toppling them over onto each other like a pack of cards.

Fuck fuck fuck says Seagrave, and he revs the Hummer as hard as it will go as a pack of big, bearded, tattooed guys in leather and denim burst out of the shadows and come running after us. The Hummer's all over the road, cars are avoiding us, I hear people screaming, especially when we ride up over the kerb and head straight for the outdoor cafe on the Macleay Street corner. People run, some fall backwards off their chairs, but at the last moment Seagrave's sawing at the wheel sends us skidding off sideways, and we go head on into the bomb-shaped El Alamein fountain, so hard the Hummer's big wheels bump us up two levels before we slam into the central pylon.

Seagrave's out and running a second later, not even looking to see if I'm all right. As he sprints off into the dark behind the public toilets, I see the bikies running after him, one of them twirling a chain, another with a beer bottle in his hand. But I don't care about Seagrave, I don't mind what they do to him, I just want out of this, but first I have to squeeze out of the Hummer, which is hard because of the angle, nose up, and as I lean out, my weight makes me plummet backwards. I slide down the fountain, through the veil of water, head first and on my back, hardly knowing what's happening, or where I am anymore. At the bottom a complete rollover dumps me onto the wet brickwork, sitting on my bum, a great big wet sodden jelly. I can't see well, there's water streaming down my face, and I think there are tears in my eyes as well, but when I look harder I realise there's a ring of people around me, staring, agitated, as if ready to hurl themselves upon me, and I hear those words again, it's Garvey Quinn, it's Garvey Quinn. Then there are other words, shame, you bastard, fuck you Quinn, how could you do that to Bryan, and an empty drink can rattles onto the brickwork near me, and then a half-full one hits me on the shoulder, and half a donut, and then a cardboard milkshake container comes wobbling through the air and gets me fair on the top of the head, chocolatey milk and ice-cream starts running down my face. That's when I start to sob, louder and louder, and nobody throws anything again, and soon some legs are in front of me, black boots and blue trousers, a policeman's voice saying, you better come with us, Quinn.

★ ★ ★

Custard.

Someone just said custard. I think of a nice big bowl of the stuff, a bowl about the size of a dustbin, thick and yellow with plenty of eggs, but no skin, that first spoonful lifting up out of it, and then another, and …

Custody.

What, I ask? That doesn't sound right.

Protective custody, the man's voice says, clearer now. Snap out of it, Quinn, this conversation's about you so you might as well take an interest in it.

I look up, through bars, and it's a policeman standing just outside, and there's a large man in a pin-striped suit, big bald-headed face. It's Alexander Morton, who seems to be cropping up everywhere these days.

Don't worry officer, I'll make sure he's just as safe as he would be if he stayed here, Morton says.

The policeman says, well sir, seeing as it's you.

Thank you officer, says Morton, and the policeman goes on, and I'd just like to say, I was very moved when you phoned up the show and apologised to Bryan like that, we were watching it here at the station, and there were quite a few tears shed, I can assure you of that.

Thank you for saying so, officer.

When I'm escorted through the back entrance and out into the yard with the high wall around it and a coil of barbed wire at the top, I'm pleased to see there's no stretch limo or Roller waiting for me, but an unobtrusive white Beemer 7 series long wheelbase, a top car but nothing anyone would look twice at, and thank Christ for the tinted windows. Apart from the policeman who's walked out with us, Morton doesn't seem to have any flunkies hanging round helping him, the way you expect really rich guys to, though when he holds the door open for me, I see that there's a chauffeur sitting waiting at the wheel, reading a newspaper. You'd think pulling the door open would have been his job.

Morton offers coffee and cake, as we pull out through the roller door, and I'm glad to accept. They offered me coffee and sandwiches at the police station, but I declined. I could see the International Roast tin across the room from my cell, and the sandwich was Tip Top sliced bread and Coon cheese, curled up at the edges, and with the whole place stinking of piss from the drunks in the cells either side of me, I just couldn't come at it. The cake that Morton gets out of the bar fridge is something else, though, thick chocolate mud cake in a box from some patisserie in Double Bay, and I seize on it, stuffing in mouthful after mouthful until it's all gone, washing it down with some of the great coffee that he pours for me out of a silver thermos. When I've finished, and wiped my mouth on an embroidered linen napkin, I'm finally ready to ask a question or two.

Mr Morton, why are you doing this for me?

It takes him a while to come up with an answer, long enough for me to pour out the rest of the coffee, but finally he says, not looking at me, some years ago I made a mistake. I thought I saw something, and I told the world what I thought I saw. But I was wrong. And that mistake totally changed someone's life. It placed on him a burden of expectation that was impossible for any human being to bear.

I wait for him to say more, but when he doesn't, I say, I understand that, but what's it got to do with helping me?

Your life was changed by my mistake too, Morton answers. Your ending up like this is part of a chain of events that began with that mistake. I created the impossible myth of Bryan Mars that led to his downfall, and without that, you never would have been cast in that unspeakable film, none of this ever would have happened.

GarVEY QUiNN

Now he does look at me for a moment, as if he's expecting me to say something, but I don't, and he goes on. That unspeakable film remains as evidence of all our mistakes. All our inadequacies as human beings.

Now I do start to see what he's after. It's only a few hours since Seagrave was trying to enlist me as the secret weapon for the defence of *Fish Out of Water*, and now Morton wants me to get up in court and speak for its destruction. I'm the meat in the sandwich.

I'm sorry, Mister Morton, I tell him. I appreciate your generosity, but if you're expecting me to get up in court and lie about anything that happened in the making of that film, I'm not prepared to do it. I've already told Stirling Seagrave the same thing.

I'm not involved in that lawsuit, Garvey, he tells me. And neither is Bryan Mars.

The car stops at some lights. The chauffeur turns round, and for the first time I see the face underneath the cap. It's Bryan, smiling back at me.

Nobody's asking you to do anything, Garvey, he tells me. But things will happen that you can't avoid, like they happen to all of us. You'll be asked to play a part, and I know you'll want to play it in the most effective way you can.

I'm completely thrown by seeing him there, and all I can think of to say is hello.

It's all up to you, Garvey, Bryan goes on. You'll be alone up there doing the best job you can, and I don't need to tell you how to completely give yourself to the role you're playing. You've already shown what you can do. And I want you to know, in spite of everything, I respect what you did. To transform yourself like that must have been just as hard as any world record swim.

StUffED

* * *

Morton sets me up in an apartment somewhere. During the drive I wasn't noticing where we were going, and all I can see from the windows are other buildings, it's all completely anonymous. That doesn't bother me, I don't have to go anywhere or do anything for a while, the place has been beautifully stocked, the fridge full of parcels from David Jones food hall, no doubt brought here by one of Morton's servants. There's so much cheese, Emmenthaler and Port-salut and gorgonzola, and some little Camemberts that will go really well deep fried. There's a big leg of Parma ham, giant salamis and a stack of those orange smoked fish, and there are also masses of chocolate biscuits wrapped up with shiny red ribbons, and a couple of chocolate cakes about the size of truck wheels. There's even a turkey, which I cook for my first dinner there, and polish off in sandwiches for lunch the next day.

Apart from cooking and eating, I don't have a lot to do except watch TV – plenty of food shows, some daytime reruns of *Medical Emergency*, but most of all the news, which within a day of my moving in is dominated by the lawsuit. Each night it's the lead story, Bryan arriving at the court and giving a little wave as he steps off his bicycle, and getting a huge cheer that goes on and on until after he's disappeared into the building. He's become so popular the police have had to lay on special crowd control measures, which could be a good thing when I finally get the call to turn up. I've already seen what happens whenever Seagrave fronts, bandaged and blackeyed and limping from when the bikies pulverised him, but defiantly giving the finger while the crowd boo and jeer. I can't see why they'll be any nicer to me – it'll be like the mob at the fountain all over again. They only let up on me when I started to cry, and I can't guarantee a repeat performance of that, not without calling for the glycerine.

What I do know is that when I finally get up there in court, whatever I say is going to make me look like a jerk in somebody's eyes, even if it's just my own. I'm not so stupid I can't see what Morton's up to, I know he's not taking care of me like this, giving me peace, protection and great food, all because he thinks I'm a nice bloke. No doubt he thinks that just like everybody else, I've got my price, and no doubt he's right. What he's hoping is that my price is the right to walk down the street again without everyone hating me, just back up Bryan and the world's love for him will rub off on me. The same goes for Seagrave's lot, of course. They think, even though their attempt to hide me out went down like a lead balloon, and even though I told Seagrave he's the lowest filth on earth and his movie isn't fit to wipe your bum on, in spite of all that I'll come through when it matters because I'm part of the industry. I'm still one of them, and just maybe one day that'll mean something to me again, and what goes round comes round.

Stuie keeps in touch, he's the only person I've given my number to, and the lawyers keep him informed about when I'm expected to be called. He's still on Seagrave's side, he doesn't have much choice, but he's stopped trying to bring me round. The couple of times when he did, I just told him to fuck off, and he didn't take it personally. It must have been Stuie who gave the number to Madeleine. It's the middle of the night when she rings.

Garvey, are you all right? she asks.

What do you think? I say. Her voice is dark and serious like it was the day she said she was leaving, and hearing it now is almost too much to bear. Yet I'm glad she's phoned.

Than she asks, what are you going to do? I say I don't know, take it as it comes. I know Madeleine hates the movie just as much as I do, but I also know she believes in the work for its own sake, and if your own truth is there in it, whatever mess anybody else makes of it, your truth stands. I'd be happy if every print of the movie was incinerated, but I can't be sure she feels the same, and everybody said she was the best thing in it.

It's all right, you can say whatever you like, she tells me. We were wrong, Garvey. Some things aren't worth transforming yourself for. You have to ask yourself, if I go that far, how will I feel if I can't come back?

It's all right for you to say that, I tell her. I remember how magnificent she looked from all that swimming, it didn't turn her into a laughing stock.

And, she goes on, you also have to ask, what if I go that far and find I don't want to come back, even though everybody says you should for the good of your career. There's something in her voice, a bit of a waver, as if it's hard to say.

I don't know what she's on about, I just know something's wrong, for her too, and I ask, Madeleine, what's going on over there?

Over where? she says.

Aren't you in Hollywood?

It doesn't matter where I am, she says.

Are you with Johnny?

Johnny's in New York, doing something for Woody, she tells me.

So he's in New York but you've stayed in Hollywood?

I can tell I'm not going to get a direct answer, and I wonder why. She just says, this isn't about me, it's about you, and I want you to know I'll be thinking about you when you get up there in court. Just do what's right for you, don't worry about anybody else. And take care, that crowd out the front looked dangerous.

Oh, I say to her, has the case been getting much coverage over there? but she doesn't respond to that.

I just want you to know I never stopped caring about you, she says, and I want to tell her the same thing, tell her this was all a mistake, but before I can she says goodbye and hangs up.

Afterwards I can't get back to sleep, I just lie there thinking of Madeleine, remembering her in so many ways. I remember a night, early in the filming, when I'd had to stop training and my transformation was about to begin, and I'd glimpsed something of the other side, I was a bit overwhelmed. By then Madeleine was really getting into the swimming, piling on the kilometres, and she'd just come back from training, she'd wrapped a sarong around her swimmers, and when she sensed my worry, she said she was in awe of what I was doing, it made her whole being tingle. That was when I reached up and peeled her sarong off her, her swimmers still wet and clinging to her, and then I slid my fingers up her thigh, and with my other hand started to peel the cossie down from the shoulders, and …

I find myself getting excited, more excited than I want to be, but then at the same time I remember myself playing fat Bryan in Darwin, stalking round the place thinking of Vicki and shoving one hand down my enormous shorts, and someone at the premiere saying, you'd wonder he could even find it. That's when I get up and put the TV on, a home shopping show, flogging a weight loss method first devised by the high priestesses of ancient Egypt and now brought to light for the first time in 4000 years. I wonder if I should phone up about it.

★ ★ ★

One night, finally, I get the call, and next morning a car turns up, sent by the producers' lawyers, who must still think I'm of use to them, but I keep them waiting for a quarter of an hour or so. I just don't want to face it, making a choice like this and making it in public. Either I turn my back on the one world that ever made me feel I might be something just a bit out of the ordinary, and what's more gave me two years with Madeleine; or I reject the forgiveness and generosity and goodwill of the man who everybody in the entire country can see is a giant compared to me. Not a fat man, but a giant, morally and ethically and spiritually, whatever you want to call it, everything that I'm not, apparently, or I wouldn't have done the movie.

Finally I can't ignore the honking horn any longer and I come down and get into the car they've sent. It's another stretch limo, unfortunately, so I'm conspicuous again, and as we approach the court I see a ripple of excitement going through the crowd as they recognise me. By the time we reach the steps, there's a throng running along behind the car, and more people spilling out over the road in front, despite a small army of police trying to keep them back. I'm worrying what they might do to me, I don't want to get out of the car, but then some of the police do push through and form a wall beside the door on my side. One of them pulls it open and I squeeze myself out. Right away I hear booing and hissing, and someone calls out, you're disgusting, you liar, and shame, fatso, shame!

Because of the mob the car's had to stop well short of the steps, so I've got a long walk, and with the booing and hissing going on and on, I'm wishing the ground would just swallow me up. But then suddenly I hear cheering from back down the road, the booing stops, and everybody turns to look. The crowd parts, as Bryan rides through on his bicycle, waving and smiling at everyone. They clear the road enough for him to ride right up to me, then he gets off the bike and hands it to some kind of court official who carries it away. There's a hush now as he walks the last few steps over to me. He hasn't stopped smiling, beaming right at me now, and then he reaches out his hand and shakes mine, in a handshake that goes on and on. When he lets go he says, we better go in, mate, there's work to do, and he gives me a pat on the back as we walk up the courtroom steps together. I'm aware of cameras still clicking, and a TV cameraman running backwards up the stairs in front of us, trying to keep us in shot all the way to the top. The steps seem to go on forever, like steps in a bad dream, and all I can do is keep dragging myself up, feeling like I'm tied to this man next to me, whose life I've somehow blundered into.

Vicki Michaels has claimed that not only was the depiction of her insulting and degrading, but that most of the film's scenes between her and Bryan simply didn't happen. According to her, there wasn't really all that much sex going on between them, they were usually too tired from training, and what did occur took place in her flat or in hotel rooms when they were competing internationally. So all the poolside bonking scenes are complete fantasy, and so is the scene where they're doing it in Bryan's BMW and drive out of the carpark with her bare bum going up and down over his lap. I never believed any of that anyway, and I'm sure Seagrave didn't either, but now when he takes the stand, I realise why Seagrave was so keen to get me on side. Seagrave's claim is that he told the story in good faith, he believed it to be true, because that's how Bryan told it to him when he went to see him up in Darwin. And I was there.

Oscar Campbell QC, acting for the producers, says to Seagrave, when you visited Mr Mars in Darwin, was it difficult to get him to tell his story?

Seagrave says, not at all. It just poured out. I think he was relieved to finally be able to tell someone about it.

So he was quite willing to talk about his relationship with Miss Michaels. Complete with all the intimate detail that's in your film?

More than willing. We couldn't shut him up. He seemed obsessed by her, kept going over and over the most intimate details of their sex life. Told us far more than we ever used in the film, if we'd put it all in the movie would have seemed like downright pornography.

As I hear this, I think, he's got a fucking nerve, and the crowd in the court thinks so too because there's a wave of sneering laughter until the judge tells them all to keep quiet. I see Bryan sitting a few rows back from me, not reacting at all to the crowd noise, still just smiling, and Alexander Morton's sitting right next to him. Campbell QC keeps the questions coming.

And his swimming career, did Mr Mars tell you much about that?

It was like getting blood out of a stone, answers Seagrave. We kept prompting him, asking him questions about his exploits in the pool, but he'd always bring it back to his relationship with Miss Michaels, he'd tell us one more lurid anecdote about what the pair of them did in a locker room, or in a shower cubicle, or in his car, whatever. When we did push him to talk about the swimming, it just seemed to make him even sadder than he already was.

So in general Mr Mars looked sad?

Depressed, you'd have to say, Seagrave answers. It was heartbreaking to see. I mean here was this enormous man, truly enormously fat man spread out on a sofa, stuffing himself with Kentucky Fried Chicken and wanting to talk about nothing except the sex life he had when he was thin.

Campbell QC says, so Mr Mars was extremely fat at that time?

Oh absolutely, says Seagrave. Gigantic. The fattest man I've ever seen.

At this there's some booing from down the back of the court, and I think I hear someone say, bullshit. Then the judge says, one more outburst like that and I'll clear the court.

Is it possible for you to give us a measure of just how fat Mr Mars was? Campbell QC asks.

Yes, says Seagrave. He was as fat as … As fat as … I duck my head, because I can see Seagrave's eyes searching over the courtroom until they land on me. He points. As fat as him over there.

Let the court record that Mr Seagrave is pointing out the actor Garvey Quinn, says Campbell QC. I think I hear somebody behind me murmur, you call him an actor? When I look round to see, I get caught directly in the gaze of Gunnar Lofgren. He's still as powerful looking as he was in his pole vaulting days, and he's got this hawkish face and deep hooded eyes. In a horror movie he'd be Dr Death or the Dark Exterminator, and he's looking straight at me, so hard it shakes me, and I have to look away. I wish these people could understand, I didn't mean to do any of this.

Next, Campbell QC calls the screenwriter, Nelson Flack, who's obviously going to agree with everything Seagrave said. Flack's still wearing that bottle green corduroy jacket, and I look hard to see if I can spot the usual dandruff flecks, though he's a bit far away. He's asked about what sort of a working relationship he had with Bryan, though it's news to me that they had any kind of working relationship at all. That definitely isn't how Flack tells it.

It was difficult, Flack says. Of course I wanted to tell the story as powerfully as possible, but I also wanted to do it with integrity, after all, I was aware that I was dealing with an iconic figure in our national mythology. But every time I discussed the script with Bryan, he'd come up with yet more sordid detail that he thought should go in, and complain that there was too much swimming. I remember one time he wanted me to put in a scene of the two of them actually doing it underwater in the pool after training.

So you kept Mr Mars fully informed about what was going into the script?

Oh, absolutely. When you're dealing with a person's life, you have to tread very carefully. And yet somehow, though he'd already sunk so low, he seemed determined to sabotage this last chance we were giving him to redeem himself in the eyes of the world. It was as if he was bent on self-destruction.

Campbell QC asks, so how did you resolve this problem?

In the end I suppose we did what we could to save Bryan from himself, Flack answers. I mean, we'd undertaken to tell his story, so we had to respect his recollection of what had happened, after all it was his life. But as Mr Seagrave said earlier, it was more a question of what we left out. For Bryan's own good.

And despite what you left out of the story, do you believe the finished film accurately reflects what Bryan told you about his relationship with Miss Michaels?

Yes I do. Absolutely. I'd stake my professional reputation on that.

GarVEY QUiNN

When I hear Flack say that I think, yeah, they'd all stake their professional reputations on the truth of absolutely everything they've ever done, even if it's just a dog food ad or a corpse on a trolley in *Medical Emergency*. And this is my world.

★ ★ ★

BRYAN MARS

You make a point of not turning round as you walk up to take the stand, you know all the people who've come there just to see you would love some acknowledgement, and this is the big, big moment, just a smile would make them so happy, but it's important you don't look as if you're putting on a show. This is for Vicki and her guy, to you the movie is just a nuisance now, but for them it must still hurt a lot, to be going through this, so you owe it to them to do the job properly. You've had a few words of advice from Alexander Morton's legal people, not that you need it, you can tell how this is going to go, after Seagrave and his mate lied through their teeth, they've paved the way for you.

Bernard Hendrickson QC asks you, Mr Mars, what details of your relationship with Miss Michaels did you disclose to the director and screenwriter of *Fish Out of Water*?

None.

Did you provide any information, of any nature, to the film makers?

No.

Were you at any stage shown a script, or told what would be in the script?

No. Not at any stage.

Mr Mars, may I ask you, how overweight were you when

the film makers came to see you in Darwin?

This is the tricky part, but you know you can get away with it. You pause, so that they can see that you're thinking, wanting to give the right answer even though it's embarrassing for you.

I was, somewhat overweight.

Hendrickson QC asks, how overweight is that, Mr Mars?

You give another thoughtful pause, then say, people may be familiar with some film taken at the time I worked as an Olympic commentator, when I disgraced myself and embarrassed the nation, something I deeply regret. The weight that I display in that news film is approximately the weight I was when the film makers met me in Darwin.

Say, about, twenty-five or thirty kilograms overweight?

About that, yes.

At this point you do glance up briefly to the gallery, and you see a few heads nodding, as if they're telling themselves, see, I knew it all along. You know what's coming next, you can tell from which way Hendrickson QC is looking.

Mr Mars, did your obesity ever approximate that of this man here, Mr Garvey Quinn?

Hendrickson QC points, as if I didn't already know where Garvey Quinn is sitting and didn't already know how big he is. The poor guy has everybody staring at him and he seems to be trying to pull himself down into his seat, his face is red and he's sweating. I take a long look, so everybody can see how seriously I'm taking this, I want even those people who spotted me in Darwin to decide their eyes must have been playing tricks on them.

No. I never resembled Mr Garvey Quinn.

As you walk back down, you can see the crowd in the courtroom can barely contain themselves, they want to give you a round of applause, they want to grab hold of you and carry you round on their shoulders. But all that can wait, you keep your eyes down as you go back to your seat, just a pat on the shoulder from Alexander Morton, and you hear him murmur, well done.

So it's all up to Garvey Quinn. You've given him plenty to work with, so now let's see what sort of an actor he is, maybe there's more to him than you'd think from watching him on the screen. The poor bastard waddles up slowly when they call out his name, and for a moment you remember what it's like to feel that way. Only for a moment though, you're getting better and better at forgetting, which is the best thing for everyone. You look around, to see how other people are reacting to him, and you see that the crowd, your fans, are stony faced, you made it easier for him this morning with the handshake and the smile, but they're a long way from forgiving him. He's got to earn that himself, and at least you've given him the chance. The director and his writer mate are looking hateful as hell as they watch him, but maybe also a bit scared, and just to make them feel even worse, when they spot you looking their way you flash them a smile.

Mr Quinn, were you present when Stirling Seagrave and Nelson Flack visited Bryan Mars in Darwin? Hendrickson QC asks.

Yes I was.

And can you tell us the nature of the conversation that took place between the film makers and Mr Mars?

You watch as Garvey Quinn does his own thoughtful pause. It's all right, but yours was better.

There wasn't any conversation, Garvey says.

Hendrickson QC asks him, none whatever?

None whatever. It was obvious he didn't want to be involved.

So at no stage did Mr Mars divulge any information about

his relationship with Vicki Michaels?

As I said, he didn't divulge anything, Garvey answers. You can see Garvey's really getting into it now, he even manages to sound annoyed at having to state the obvious.

So can you tell us what did transpire in the meeting with Mr Mars?

Nothing, Garvey answers, like you want him to. He goes on, Bryan just sat there, his mother showed us a scrapbook with all the old photos of Bryan, most of which we'd seen already, and then we left.

When you hear him mention your mum you're glad she's well out of this, on a cruise ship somewhere off the Alaskan coast. Garvey's stopped sweating, and the redness has gone from his face. He looks almost eager to hear the next question, and when Hendrickson QC asks him where the idea for all the sex scenes came from, he jumps right in.

Mr Seagrave and Mr Flack came up with the idea on the plane going back. They had a magazine with an old picture of Vicki Michaels in it, from an Olympic calendar where she was, um, nude.

You look round and you see Vicki looking downwards, and Gunnar shooting Garvey with those killer eyes. Garvey goes on.

Mr Seagrave and Mr Flack were really getting off on the picture. Then Mr Seagrave said to Mr Flack, what are you like at writing sex scenes? And Mr Flack said he could write them with one hand. He said that was how he preferred to write them.

There are a few sniggers around the court, until the judge says, quiet please!

There's one final matter I'd like to ask you about, says Hendrickson QC. When you saw Mr Mars that time in Darwin, was he as, shall we say, large as you are now?

Garvey doesn't hesitate. No. Nothing like me, he says.

So if the real person you'd been asked to play was not of your present size, why did you choose to put on so much weight?

At this, Campbell QC jumps in with an objection.

We're here to consider the accuracy of the film's depiction of Mr Mars's relationship with Miss Michaels, not to discuss an actor's obesity problem.

The judge isn't standing for this though. He says, I think it would be enlightening for us all to know more about how Mr Quinn came to acquire his present physical stature. Please continue Mr Hendrickson.

Hendrickson QC asks again, Mr Quinn, why exactly did you choose to put on so much weight?

The question seems to throw Garvey, at least for a moment, and you see him looking around, as if he's wishing someone could help him. There'll be no help from Seagrave, who looks like he wants to kill him.

Then Garvey's blank look goes, and he says, because they told me to.

Hendrickson QC looks a bit puzzled by this. They just told you to do this to yourself, and you did?

I'm an actor, says Garvey. The part I was playing was this big, so I got this big.

But Bryan Mars was not that big, says Hendrickson.

Yes, but the character in the script was, answers Garvey. That's who I was playing, not the real Bryan Mars.

So you felt you had to become the character as presented to you in the script, no matter what the consequences? says Hendrickson QC.

Yes, answers Garvey. That's just part of my job. That's what I do. The truth doesn't come into it, even though everybody says it does, and they all know it doesn't.

StUffED

Hendrickson QC stares at Garvey for a few moments, screwing up his eyes, then says, so, you're saying that you'll go along with whatever turns up in the script that's offered to you, and call it the truth just because everybody else does?

I suppose so, yes.

Mr Quinn, do you think that's really a very sensible thing to do?

No. It's completely stupid. Just really, really stupid.

★ ★ ★

Garvey Quinn

For an enormously fat man, I became surprisingly invisible once I'd given my evidence. For a day or two afterwards, people kept up the waving and cheering and the, good on you Garvey, they'd carried on with when we walked out of the courtroom together like a couple of heroes. But there was only room for one hero and obviously that was Bryan, that was obvious to me on that first evening. While we were in public, with the crowd around, and cameras, I lost count of the number of pats on the back I got from him, the number of extra handshakes and big generous smiles, we were lifelong friends, brothers in arms. But then in the underground carpark, after Bryan had slung his bike into the boot of Alexander Morton's Roller, and I tried to say a few parting words, it was like Bryan wasn't there anymore.

Well Bryan, I just wanted to say that you've been very understanding about all this, and I hope that what I did today has in some way helped to make amends, it's been a difficult time for everybody, and I admire the way you've …

And that was where I left it, I could see he wasn't listening, all that radiant goodwill had just disappeared from his face like he'd turned off a switch. He didn't even look back at me as he slammed the door of the Rolls, and I looked away at the same moment. I could understand of course, why would he want to spend a moment longer than necessary looking at someone who was the image of what he once was, but now denied ever having been? From now on I was the image only of myself, the old fat Bryan wouldn't even exist on film anymore, because along with paying Vicki Michaels and the pole vaulter substantial damages, the producers had been ordered to destroy all copies of *Fish Out of Water*.

And good riddance. It might have been the biggest performance I ever gave, but compared even to *Medical Emergency*, it was crap. At least in *Medical Emergency* you could still see Garvey Quinn in there somewhere; in *Fish Out of Water* you wouldn't know who you were looking at, and you wouldn't care. In fact, if I had to pick out a single performance I'm genuinely proud of, where the real me shone through, it would have to be up there in the courtroom. An audience of millions, no contract, no script, no director, just a big fat bloke saying what was on his mind. I had them eating out of my hand, and from then on, I knew, I'd never have to listen to anybody telling me about the truth ever again.

I was also free to walk the streets if I felt like it, relatively unchallenged, just an occasional, good on you Garvey, but mostly left alone. I'd done my bit, but I wasn't an important part of the Bryan Mars story anymore, and I wasn't interesting as a movie star gone wrong, either, it seemed as if the public had run out of fat jokes. Nor did I cop the recrimination I feared from the movie industry either, partly I suppose because I wasn't looking for a job so there wasn't much they could do to me, but partly I suspect because everybody thought Seagrave was such a bastard and he got what he deserved. The last I heard of him was that he'd got himself a gig in Amsterdam directing some low-budget, direct-to-cable all-nude feature called *The Bottomless Pit*.

Garvey Quinn

A day after the case I moved back in with Dad, not because I particularly wanted to, but because I had nowhere else to go. Just after I got up that morning, a couple of security guards turned up to tell me that I was no longer welcome in the apartment, Mr Morton had pulled the plug. Back home, though I was now able to go out without anyone bothering me, I rarely went further than the front gate. I had no reason to go anywhere except to shop for food. That was necessary because Dad was well and truly sticking to his resolve not to help me anymore. He seemed to be about the one person in the entire country who wasn't won over by what I'd done in the courtroom. So every couple of days I'd waddle up the road to the nearest convenience store and come back with as much as I could possibly carry, exorbitantly priced compared to the supermarket, but I just didn't seem to have it in me to organise going further than a few blocks.

I stopped being adventurous with the cooking, too, I'd just cook it up in the easiest possible way, shovel it in, and wait until it was time for the next meal, doing nothing much, and not enjoying the anticipation either. The next meal would be just like the last, nothing exciting or interesting, just necessary. If there'd been a moment of expectation of a new life when I was up on the stand and made that decision to assist in the killing off of the film that had made me like this, that expectation was long gone. Then one day Stuie rang, for the first time since before the court case.

How's it going? Stuie asks me.

How do you reckon? I say to him.

I told you not to do it, Garvey. What you did was great for Bryan Mars but it did fuck all for you.

I tell him angrily, I did the right thing, Stuie, I did what I had to do, I wasn't expecting miracles afterwards. Now if you don't mind, I'm busy cooking my lunch.

Come on, says Stuie, you can't just go on like that.

Can't I?, I ask him. Have you got a better idea?

As a matter of fact I have, he says. There's a ray of hope in all this.

Yeah?

This morning I had a brainwave, Stuie tells me. Ever watched a show called, *A Weight off your Mind*?

Heard about it. People call it the fat show, don't they?

The fat show, exactly. Anyway, it's got big sponsorship from a weight loss company, Bulk Busters International, basically it's infotainment. And what they do is, they get people, fat people, onto the show, and they bring people back, week after week, month after month, and gradually try to get the weight off them.

I tried losing weight, Stuie, remember Gerda Busch, the best in the business?

I don't think Gerda Busch had ever dealt with someone as far gone as you, says Stuie. She bit off more than she could chew, so to speak. But these people are different, they don't cut your food down to nothing and try to work your arse off the way she did, they've got psychiatrists working for them, and they'll put you in hospital for a while if need be, so they can observe how you …

Did you say psychiatrists?

Yes. Psychiatrists. Somebody had to say it.

And you think I'd do all this in public? Are you completely fucking crazy?

Stuie explains, that's the whole point, the producers told me. Once somebody gets as far as appearing on the show, they're too embarrassed not to go back, to let the world know they've given up. Fear of public failure is what gets people going, apparently.

Do you think the public hasn't already seen enough of my failure?

For Christ's sake Garvey, what have you got to lose? Except about half a ton? Is it going to make your life any worse than it is already? People already know what you look like. They don't shoot it with an audience or anything. They just pick you up every week, take you in there, film you getting weighed, film you eating, and show you working out for a couple of minutes, and the rest is done completely in private.

But what if I just can't do it?

They've had great results. And when I told them the idea of you going on the show, they jumped at it. They've never had such a challenge before, and they're ready to do absolutely anything they can for you, because it'll make them look so good if they can make it happen. What's more, people won't be laughing at you, Garvey, if you do it they'll be saying how brave you are, for some misguided reason they already think you were brave getting up there in court and doing what you did.

It all sounds great, but so much has happened already I don't know how to decide anything anymore, and I tell Stuie, like I said to Seagrave when he offered me the job, I'll think about it.

Yeah, yeah, I know you're cautious, he says. And you've got reason to be. But there's got to be more to your life than this, hasn't there? There's got to be life after Bryan Mars.

I don't have anything to say to that. Stuie tells me they want an answer by tomorrow, and I agree to at least take a look at tonight's episode of the fat show.

While I wait for the show to come up, I cook what's easiest, just a mountain of eggs and bacon, I know it's not breakfast time but it always goes down well. Then I channel surf, and find they're replaying the first series of *Medical Emergency*. I know that series so well, it was the first big thing I was in and I used to play it over and over again on video, I could hardly believe it was happening, so even now, four years later, I'm saying every line, not just mine, but everybody else's. I wait for the scene to come up where this woman rushes in carrying a kid who's been making rockets in the garden shed and blown himself to smithereens. He's still breathing, just, and she's hysterical, more so when she finds that the only doctor on duty is tied up trying to save an off-duty constable with a bullet in his brain. I've just knocked off after an eighteen-hour shift, and as I often did in the show, I'm unwinding with a bit of a jog in the park. A nurse comes after me, that busty one, Lisa, who I was always trying to crack onto until I met Madeleine, and she summons me back, and I operate on the kid just with a theatre gown thrown over my running gear, which probably broke every hygiene regulation in the book, but shit I looked good. At the end I say, well, I've made sure he's going to live, the rest is up to the plastic surgeons.

I wasn't bad, you know, looking back on it now, I wasn't bad at all. I'm starting to think, maybe they could do something for me, and wouldn't it be a good angle for their show if they now and again showed clips of me in *Medical Emergency*, just to show what I'm aiming at. Then the fat show comes on, and it's just as bad as I remember from the few minutes I've ever seen, the people are clumsy and hopeless, they've obviously had their lines scripted for them, but they haven't got the first clue about delivery. I think to myself, I could do ten times better than that!

★ ★ ★

GARVEY QUINN

The producers sent someone to pick me up and then drop me home, now in discreet vans rather than those stupid stretch limos, and after the first few times I lost some of my embarrassment in the weigh-in scene which is always the opener. I had to strip down to these gigantic satin boxer shorts they'd had made for me, and climb onto the scales, special ones they'd got from an abattoir supplier. I'd have to stand there, my flesh wobbling and the scales groaning, while a tape measure was run round my waist. One person would hold the end of the tape on my belly button while the other person would walk round me unrolling the tape until they got back to the starting point.

The rest of the show, thankfully done with my gear back on, consisted of scenes of me talking seriously to an obesity counsellor about getting back in touch with my thinner child, as somebody called it, plus scenes of me eating and exercising. The eating wasn't so bad, reasonable sized portions of the sort of food I liked, instead of trying to cut me back to nothing, and the exercise was just gentle walking on a treadmill.

In a few weeks I'd lost enough for them to be able to superimpose before and after shots and see a difference. There wasn't much difference, just enough for one silhouette to be a snug fit inside the other, but at least it was something. Within a few months, though, enough had come off for them to have had to make two lots of progressively smaller boxer shorts for the weigh-in. I was turning into just an ordinary very very fat man, rather than a freak, the sort of fat man who might need a whole bus seat to himself, but wouldn't actually break the seat. So I could get around a bit more, I bought myself an old Landcruiser and had the seat remounted a few inches further back. When I was out, nobody really seemed to notice me, just the odd kid shouting out hey fatso, and probably not even knowing who I was anyway. I got myself some new gear, too, from the Big Men's shop. I found that their very largest clothes just fitted me, with a bit of squeezing in, and I was able to burn the stuff that Auntie Janice had made. It now seemed possible that, at this rate of progress, in a couple of years I might not be too far away from looking the way I used to.

Then they axed *A Weight off your Mind*. When Stuie broke it to me he said, the ratings were down, it seems as if there wasn't enough action, there's only so much excitement you can squeeze out of watching someone's stomach get smaller. Sorry Garvey, but at least you gave it your best shot.

At first I was shattered. I just lay around eating, and when I did force myself to go out, I doubled the size of the shopping list, back to the way it was before. Somehow, though, I couldn't get through it as fast as I thought I would, there seemed a limit to how much I could pig out now.

Then, a few days after he hit me with the bad news, Stuie phones again. He says, I think I've got something for you. Best thing for you is to get back into the business instead of moping around all day. I give Stuie an answer right away, without even thinking.

I'll do it. Whatever it is.

That's the boy, Stuie says. By the way, Madeleine sends her love.

Love? I want to ask, did she really say, tell Garvey I'm still in love with him? Or did she just say, give him my love? But you can't ask questions like that.

So, she's back? I just say.

That's right.

With Johnny?

Apparently not. I hear things didn't work out. Not with him and not with anything else. She came into my office to collect all her files and publicity photographs. Said she was going to burn them, she's getting out of the business.

I ask Stuie, So what's she doing now?

Swimming, mostly.

I try to get an address or a contact number out of Stuie but he doesn't have one.

If she wanted people to know where she is, she'd have said so, he tells me.

I'm stunned by the news. How could Madeleine give up the thing that was her whole reason for existence? And which she was so good at. But then I remember what she said on the phone in the middle of the night: What if you transform yourself into someone else and then don't want to go back? Is that what's happened to her? Does the Madeleine I knew even exist anymore? Stuie's noticed how hard it's hit me.

Get over it. Get on with the next role. You're an actor, aren't you? That's what you do.

What Stuie had lined up was a role in a sitcom, *Tight Squeeze*, about a shared household. My character was called Tiny Tubkins, and he was a big fat guy who never left the kitchen, he was in there all day cooking and eating, so the other members of the household could never get in, he took up so much space. He was a sort of one joke character, but it worked, I enjoyed playing him, and I got plenty of laughs. What was also great was that they let me do the cooking scenes for real. After all that I'd turned into quite a good cook, and at the end of shooting the cast and crew would have a big blow-out on whatever I hadn't eaten during the show. I found everybody liked me, and what's more the show started rating sky high.

Then as a spin-off, I got offered my own cooking show, *Tiny's Kitchen*. I got given some lessons in TV cooking, not just throwing it together like I did in *Tight Squeeze*, and had some help expanding my repertoire, but basically all I had to do was go in there and be myself. Ratings were good, they still are, and *Tight Squeeze* is going into another series, there are *Tiny's Kitchen* cookbooks with me on the cover, and I'm often stopped in the street. I'm back in my flat now, and just about any time I walk round to one of the cafes, somebody'll come up and say, I loved it when they played a joke on you by putting a live pig in the fridge and you got back at them by cooking nothing but pork all week and pretending it was from the pig they'd brought, or, I cooked that Beef Wellington you did on the show, and gee it was great, or, at last I know how to cook Vietnamese duck. They always look happy when they come up and talk to me, and usually they're fat, as fat as me.

But if there's a lot of me on television, it's nothing to how much Bryan Mars there is, just about any time you turn it on. He's got his own adventure show, *Bryan Mars's World of the Deep*, and this time nobody jokes about calling it Bryan Mars Plumbs the Depths. It's big budget stuff, they show him going all over the world, diving in with all sorts of sea creatures, making funny noises at them as if he's talking to them. He's also got his own chat show, *Tonight with Bryan Mars*, and they bring on all these guests who are supposed to be deep thinkers, though mostly it just seems like an excuse for Bryan to philosophise about being at one with the life force.

The show rates through the roof, though I can rarely bring myself to watch it. One time when I do, though, I find myself wondering why the woman sitting next to him in the guest chair is familiar. She's in some kind of a team tracksuit, she's broad shouldered, a swimmer, her hair in almost a crew-cut, intense, there to talk about nothing but swimming. She's introduced as the new record-breaking sensation, Maralyn Hollis, but it's not, it's Madeleine.

GARVEY QUINN

She looks comfortable with Bryan Mars, looking him in the eye a lot, like she knows he understands, the way she used to look at me when she talked about acting, but I don't feel jealous, because there's not much of my Madeleine left. There are no questions about where she's come from, what she used to be, just swimming, swimming, swimming. She talks about how she got the record, how she swam the first four laps faster than the second four, how much that hurts but it's what you have to do. There's the pain of the last lap, she says, the oxygen debt, your muscles have used up all their lactic acid, at the end you feel you could die. Literally, you feel you could die.

But, says Bryan, you know you won't.

No, agrees Madeleine, or whoever she is now, I won't. Next time I'll go beyond that, pain is only psychological, it's within us to do anything.

Then they go on about the next record in her sights, that record is soft, she says, there's four seconds to come out of it, but if I dig deep, I believe I'm almost there. Bryan agrees, it's between you and the stopwatch, and she says, that's why I swim, because it's between me and the clock, I can measure absolutely what I've done, there's no room for illusion, it doesn't matter what I say or what I think, the truth is there in black and white. Either I get the record or I don't.

That's where I turn it off. I've never been that interested in sport, even less so now, and this Maralyn I'm looking at seems like just another swimmer, though I wish her well.

Bryan Mars, though, isn't just another swimmer. As well as his shows, every time Bryan breaks another long distance swimming record, which is often, you get masses of coverage of that. He's smashed the English Channel record five times, knocked hours off Miami to Havana, swum from Greece to Italy, and now he's tuning up for Bass Strait.

Somehow in the middle of all this he finds time to marry Maralyn Hollis, underwater, in the middle of a pod of dolphins. He looks sleeker than ever, sleeker even than when he was an Olympic contender, and always he's got that glowing smile. He's got so popular there's even talk of another movie being made about his life, but this time Bryan will play himself.

I'm sure he'll do a better job than I did. But I won't be going to see it.